I0550224

CHAPTER ONE

HOW IT STARTED

The school principal suspended me for three days.

"Benjamin," my mom said, "you are too young to smoke. Besides you shouldn't smoke at any age."

"Fourteen isn't too young." I reminded her.

"How would you know?"

"I know I want to try things."

"Things?" she gasped. "Well try your room. You are grounded for three days."

"How about giving me a time out instead?"

In my room

You now know my first name, age, and you met my mother. My room isn't all that large but it is comfortable, with a bed, desk, chair and window seat where I keep my telescope. The closet had sliding doors behind which hung my clothes, next to a wall of drawers. Behind the drawers a door hid most of my secrets. Mom didn't know about the panel dividing the shelf from front to back.

Above this shelf, a panel lifted into the attic. Everyone thought it was the

entrance to a dusty room of rafters and insulation, which was true, only this

dusty place led to another room. It was my best secret of all, especially

considering what was in that room.

The Church Bazaar

Mom worked the swing shift at the phone company. It was Saturday, her

day off, so she let me wander around the village. One of her rules had me

check in with her every two hours. It was every hour until I was fourteen.

"You can't get very far on your bike in one hour." She would say.

On my fourteenth birthday she bought me a new bike. It cost over two

hundred dollars.

My Grandmother, who lived in Oregon, helped her pay for it. Grandmother was

my father's mom. My father lived in Las Vegas. He left us when I was six years

old. Each summer Mom sent me to visit Grandmother. One time I asked my

Grandmother why my father left us all alone. She told me to ask my mom.

When I did, all mom would say was that he was a drunk. For many years I did

not know what a drunk was until I met this boy in fifth grade. We were both held

2

back a year in school. Being older than the other students Josh and I became close friends. Very close friends are hard to find.

On the Saturday of the bazaar Josh was grounded. His younger brother Mikey told their mother that Josh took some cigarettes from her purse. I went to the bazaar alone not telling my mother that on the new bike I could get pretty far, but there was no *sense* pushing it, as the two hour check in time was one of my birthday presents.

An Irish band was playing outside of the doors to the school. The church common was set up with booths and tables. The usual food was being sold; hot dogs, French fries, cakes and pies from the baking contest and ice cones. One of the booths in the bazaar surprised me. A man was selling books.

Surprise because just about all the booths were craft items or carnival type junk. Surprise because I love books. Math was not a favorite subject of mine but reading was. Many of my books were kept in the secret room. Mom started looking through my books when Grandfather began sending them to me. If she did not approve of a book, which Grandfather sent, she took it from me. Josh got magazines from his mother's boyfriend. Mom would never approve of those in a million years. When I was twelve, Grandfather sent me "Catcher in the Rye." Mom would not let me read it as it was on the unapproved list in our

school library. What mom did not know is that after that when the mail came, I,

being the only one home, hid the books grandfather sent. They were put behind

the shelf above the drawers in the closet. By thirteen there were too many

books to hide. That is when I discovered the entrance to the attic. It was easy

to hide the books there under the insulation. One afternoon, in the attic, I found

the hidden room. Mom came close to discovering my secret stash.

The bazaar suddenly took on a new meaning for me. It was magical.

Approaching the book stand I saw a large jar. People were putting tickets in the

jar as I watched. The man behind the book table spoke to me.

"Would you like a chance to win a free try for the 'Webster's New World

Dictionary'," He asked me.

Would I? Wanting nothing more at the moment, my hands trembled as I

filled out the information. As I placed the ticket in the jar, I asked the man,

"When is the drawing?"

"Five o'clock." He replied. "I have to be home by then." I told him.

He chuckled. "If your ticket is drawn we will call you."

"I can't put my phone number on the ticket, just my name. My mother won't let me give out the number to anyone."

"What is your name?"

"Benjamin."

"Then Benjamin, if your name is drawn you may come to the bookstore and claim your prize."

My heart lifted. "What bookstore?"

He gave me a card. The store was located on the main street of the village. "Come and see me Monday after school."

Now I can tell you I knew every store on the main street, but never saw a bookstore.

There is magic, things like hope and believing, joy in finding new things, new people we meet in our lives, excitement beyond Christmas and Birthdays. Books did that to me.

Then, it was time to go home. I was sure to ride my new bike to the main street tomorrow in search of the store. My hope for the large 'New World Dictionary' began many adventures, the best of which led to the discovery of yet another secret room in the attic.

Having found the store closed on Sunday my anticipation grew all through

Monday and it seemed like the final school bell would never ring to end the

school day.

It also seemed that I grew a little older that day, stronger and less worried

about my world. I felt more rebellious, throwing caution aside knowing in my

heart there was nothing to lose by changing things around in my world, a world

without my father.

CHAPTER TWO

Officer Sherwood

The next day I asked my friend Josh to go to the Bookstore with me. He was still grounded. His mother told him she was in trouble with the police. The village police caught her with the boyfriend and some pot. They were smoking in his car outside a bar on the main street. Now Josh's mom did not want to get arrested and risk having her two boys taken away. She was on probation and both Josh and Mikey were in protective custody. This is what Josh told me.

"What is protective custody?" I asked him.

"The county looks out for us since my mom left Mikey and me home by ourselves." Josh replied.

"How did they find out? My mom leaves me alone when she works." I told him.

"Yeah, but your neighbor downstairs looks out after you until your mom gets home from work."

"So, how did they find out?" I asked.

"One night Mikey and I stayed out late. We were running through the cemetery when this police officer caught us. He told us we were breaking the village curfew. When he asked us where we lived, he took us home and mom

wasn't there. She was at the bar with Eric, her latest boyfriend. Mikey told the

police where she was. She always told us where she would be in case of

trouble. Then she had to go to court and the county put us on protective

custody. Each week a social worker comes to talk to me Mikey and Mom. Not

long after that, the policeman showed up at our place. It was late at night. Mom

asked him what he was doing here. He told her his name was Officer Sherwood

and that he just stopped by to see if she was OK. They sat at the

kitchen table, drinking coffee and smoking cigarettes.

 Mikey and I were in the next room listening.

 Sherwood stayed that night and slept with our mom. To Mikey and me he

was just another boyfriend."

 "My mom hates men." I said.

 "We live on welfare and mom can't pay the bills on the check she gets

from the county. She always needs a boyfriend to get by on." Josh said.

 "You and your brother must hate that."

"We did at first. Now we get along with Eric. He buys us the Playboy Magazines and we get to watch the adult videos when he is sleeping. Mikey steals his cigarettes and he lets us smoke them."

"What about Officer Sherwood. What does Eric think of him?"

"He doesn't know about him. Eric works nights at the foundry and goes out drinking in the morning when he is done working. Sherwood stays over only once or twice a month. We know better than to tell Eric. If he left mom we would have to put up with another boyfriend. Eric leaves us alone and he isn't mean."

"What is Officer Sherwood like?"

"Mikey and I don't like him very much if that's what you mean. After the first night he slept in bed with mom, he saw me on the street the next day and stopped me as I was riding my bike. He wanted to know how I was doing. I told him fine. He looked different in the daytime. He has a thin moustache that looks like it was painted under his nose."

"What is your mother doing today?" I asked Josh.

"She is home watching a movie with Eric, and I had to leave the house." Josh said.

"When Officer Sherwood stopped me I was in the Village Park." I told

Josh, " He put his arm around my shoulder. I pulled away from him.

Sherwood stood up and turned toward me so I could see his gun. He put

his hand on top of the holster, playing with the handcuffs on his other side.

"Tell me Josh," he asked me,. "Doesn't your brother work at the bookstore

on the corner?"   "He runs errands

and stuff."   "Is that all

he does there?" Sherwood smiled. It was not a good smile. "Do you

know anything about the man who owns the store? How much does he

pay your brother for those errands?"

"Why are you asking me?" I didn't want to answer more of his questions.

"What does your brother say about him?"

"Ask him." I said. "I wanted to walk away but Sherwood blocked my path

to the street."

"Don't get smart with me you little punk. One call to the county services

and your mom will be back in court." He growled.

"What for, sleeping with a cop?" It was the wrong thing to say to Officer

Sherwood.

"He grabbed me by the top of my shirt and would have lifted me off the ground except my shirt slipped over my head. Quickly I pulled my arms out of the shirt and stood there bare from the waist up with Sherwood holding an empty shirt."

"Wow. Then what happened?" I tried to imagine me being in Josh's place. "Did you run? I would have."

"I would have Ben except a strange thing happened. The man from the bookstore stepped beside me and looked Officer Sherwood in the eyes. He came out of nowhere, I swear."

"Maybe he was in the bushes behind you." I told him.

"Maybe, but when Sherwood saw him the cop let out a low growl, threw down the shirt and walked away."

"Did you tell anyone else about this?"

"Only Mikey knows about it and now you Benjamin. That is how I got to know the man in the bookstore."

"What happened next?"

"He picked up my shirt and helped me put it on. I was confused. It seemed my mind was spinning around like my feet were off the ground.

Then like some kind of dream when you wake up and feel safe, you wish

you could do it all over again, like reach your arms up and let your mother

slide your Tee Shirt on. I wished he could do it again. Like you said Ben,

there will never be a first time once it happens."

"My grandfather told me there is a first time for everything. We just

need to let it happen." I don't know why I said that. Grandfather says

many things which don't make sense until later, when they happen. It is

as though he knows how my mind works, then goes about putting an idea

in the right place at the right time."

It was then, that I felt, that this bookstore was a magic place for me.

It would be a way, from where I was, to where I was going. Grandfather

told me the secret room was to be my next dimension.

I did not know what Grandfather was talking about, until Monday after school.

CHAPTER THREE

A Bell Jingled

The first thing to do when I get home from school was to call Mom at work. Today I went into the bathroom with one of Josh's magazines. When I finished I called her. She asked me how school was and did I have any homework. When I told her no, she reminded me that my teacher gave homework assignments every day. She let us do it in class was my reply. It was math and a reading assignment. We were reading "Call of The Wild," a story by Jack London which was in my bookcase because it wasn't banned in the school library. It was a good story and I had read it twice since Grandfather sent it to me last year. As for the math I wasn't sure the answers were right but all of the problems were done. As I said, math was not one of my favorite subjects, especially algebra. This was soon to change, though I did not know it then.

"Be careful when you go out honey. There is goulash in the fridge. Warm it in the Microwave for three minutes. Don't leave your bike unlocked even in the park. And Ben don't...."

"Yes mom. I know. Don't forget to call you in two hours." It was the same everyday. Only the menu for supper changed. I ran down to the garage to get my bike and to tell Mrs. Fontana where I was going.

"Do you want some cookies and milk?" She asked.

"Thanks but no Mrs. Fontana. Maybe when I come back from the park I'll be hungry." I had to go through the park to get downtown. It was time to go to the bookstore. As anxious as I was to get there my feet pedaled slowly. My mind was going much faster. When I reached the park a police car drove by. The cop looked at me. It had to be Sherwood with the mustache painted under his nose. He wore dark glasses, hiding his eyes, surely the man who slept with Jason's mother. Finally, reaching the bookstore, my heart beat faster as the lock snapped around my bike.

The window of the store was filled with books, hundreds of them, most with the spines showing except for one row in the front that displayed their front covers. There in the center of the row was 'Catcher in The Rye.' The sun behind me came out of the clouds filling the window with bright light. Suddenly I wasn't sure of anything, whether I wanted to go inside, maybe cruise around the sidewalks or go home.

My wanting to win the dictionary won out in the end. Slowly I opened the door and walked inside. A bell jingled above me continuing to ring as the large door closed behind me. My eyes could hardly believe what they saw. My brain danced along the rows of shelves reaching up to the tall ceiling, shelves of books going far into the rear of the shop. Never had I seen so many books, more than the school library, more than in my favorite movie, "Unending Story" where a boy about my age found a magical book and then set out on many adventures. It seemed my adventures would be greater than his, that there would no end to the travels ahead of me. I had stepped into another world far from the street outside. Mikey had to be one of the luckiest boys in town, or the world, maybe even the universe. The bookman was standing behind a glass oak counter.

"Benjamin." He seemed really pleased to see me.

"Did I win?"

"No. Sorry. Some lady from the church drew the ticket for the prize."

The child in me grew sad for I wanted that dictionary more than all the books in this store, though the older me understood. When I was eight years old giving up asking about my father, Grandfather held me by the hand walking me to the dark side of the house under the Oregon Sky. "Benjamin. There are untold stars blinking above us, below us, around us. He pointed out the constellations, which I came to know from the telescope in my room. His gift was not only the telescope. Eventually he sent me star charts and maps of the sky. In the lonely hours of night, as Mom worked, I learned the coordinates and such words as ascension and declination, how any object in the sky can be found by drawing lines around a celestial sphere. This information was kept from everyone even Jason who had his own lines drawn in his head by the many boy friends his mother slept with. Mikey's father was in prison. When I asked if he wrote to him he told me no, that Mikey would send him a letter on his birthday. It was never answered. Mikey was too young to be abused by his father and no one told him his father was forbidden to see or write his son. Jason told me he was not going to tell Mikey any of this.

Standing there thinking of my Grandfather filled my heart with longing for when he held my hand so long ago. I put my backpack on the floor and walked along the rows of books.

What seemed like a few minutes became hours, time spent without me reaching the end of the store shelves. It was time to call Mom. If I called her when I got home it would be too late to meet the deadline.

Picking up my pack I started rushing out of the store.

"Do you want to call her from the store?" He asked.

Looking stupid I stood there by the door as he handed me the phone. When I called her, Mom told me to clean out the center of the garage, thinking I was home. Saying goodbye to her, I handed him the receiver.

"How did you know I was supposed to call my mom?"

"I figured it out. You kept looking at your watch on Saturday. Today you looked at books and not your watch. Then you started rushing out of here.

You mentioned your mom at the church yard so two and two equals a mom somewhere waiting for a call."

"Thanks. I'll ask her if I can come back tomorrow."

"Don't forget your backpack." He opened the door for me as the bell jingled above us.

Meeting Officer Sherwood

When I reached the garage there was a police car waiting in the driveway. Something must be wrong with Mrs. Fontana. Riding around to the back of the house Mrs. Fontana called to me. Standing next to her was Officer Sherwood. He removed his glasses as he stood looking at me.

"This policeman is asking about you Benjamin." She told me.

"What is he doing here?" I asked, really surprised to see him at my place.

"He wants to ask you some questions Benjamin."

He introduced himself. Sure enough it was Sherwood. "Where is your mother?" he asked.

"She's at work."

"What time does she get home?"

"Tonight, she works the second shift. Why?" I asked

"I ask the questions." He told me. "Who takes care of you?"

"You're looking at her officer, Mrs. Fontana here."

"But you are alone in your apartment and not down here with her. Isn't that right?" He asked.

"Has my mother done something wrong?" I asked him. I know I hadn't.

"Maybe she has and maybe she hasn't." He replied.

"So?" was all I could think to say to him.

"So! Have her call me tomorrow after 12 noon." He handed me a card with his name and phone number on it, along with village police logo.

When I took the card from him he stood there looking me up and down. "Kind of young to be hanging alone, aren't you?"

Bells jingled in my head like the ones above the door at the bookstore. About to defend myself, and answer him, all that came out of me was, "Yes sir."

He left and Mrs. Fontana fed me some cookies and milk. After cleaning the garage and putting things away I went upstairs. In my room it was time for a safety check, in order not to leave anything forbidden where mom could find it. Since the beginning of the year my backpack had a condom hidden in a pencil case. Jason gave it to me when he found some in Eric's pants. He was looking for cigarettes and the condoms were an extra bonus.

"What if he screws your Mom, can't find a rubber and gets her pregnant?" I asked Josh.

"Mom's on the pill." He replied.

"What if she forgets to take it? He screws her without one and she has a baby? You will have another little brother or sister. She could have twins, one for you and one for Mikey."

Josh laughed. "I don't think so Ben. It happened once and she had herself scraped clean before a baby could come."

Reaching into my backpack another surprise waited for me, or rather three of them. I dumped the books on the floor. The Bookman had to have put them there while I was looking through the store. The first was 'Catcher in The Rye; Second; Dimensional Calculus; Third, and strangest of all; Architecture of the Victorians; Questions flooded inside my head. How did he know about 'Catcher'? What did Dimensional Calculus have to do with me who didn't even like Algebra? The real mystery, the one that started the whole journey ahead of me was the book on Victorian Architecture. I opened it first.

On page one of the textbook the person writing the book talked about how nineteenth century houses were designed to hide rooms. My room was on the third floor where a round window stood out beneath a cone shaped roof overhead. I learned later that it was called a cupola. More surprises waited for me. I turned the page and saw a drawing of the house where I lived. It had the same style, with the round window and cone roof pictured in the book.

My next surprise came when looking out of the window of the cupola. My nights were spent here searching for the stars. I spotted Officer Sherwood and his patrol car parked across the street. Fixing my telescope on him, I could see that he sat looking toward my house. His thin moustache did look like it was painted on. I was above the trees with a view of the Southwestern sky. It was here, charting the heavens over the little village in upstate New York that my journey began.

Getting rid of Officer Sherwood was easy. Going down the back stairs and into the garage, it took it took two connections to Mrs. Fontana's phone box to report a fire on the other side of the village.

Back in my room there was a book waiting to be explored. The next page had the drawings of the floor plans that turned out to be the same as our house. It was not easy for me to figure out which room was mine. When I did, it was easy to see that my room was located under the third floor drawings beneath the attic space. This was the secret room waiting to be discovered. Tonight was cloud covered, so there no stars to watch, leaving me free to poke and probe in the dusty attic. I really will need a shower tonight. Before I was twelve showers

were a real problem. No longer, since I met Josh.

CHAPTER FOUR

My Priest

When my twelfth birthday arrived the mailman delivered a card from my

Grandfather. Turning twelve wasn't such a big deal for I wanted to be a

teenager. Twelve was just not enough for me. Josh was thirteen and it seemed

better for me to be the same age as him.

Since my telescope arrived, all my discoveries in the skies were recorded

in what I called my Astronomy Maps or Map Logs. Along with the charts my

notes were written on the feelings and discoveries of my own world. Most of the

things my grandfather told me were entered in the Maps book. Remember how

I mentioned earlier that many of his sayings were not something making sense

to me at the time? On my visit last summer he looked through my Maps book.

He took me for a walk in the forest. We came across a large pond. Above us

water poured from a bank of rocks into the pond. We walked behind the falls

and entered a large cave. The sound of water over the rocks was softer. The

high ceiling of the cave could not be seen. Grandfather sat on a log. Unlike the

moss on other logs, which floated into this cave over the years, the one he sat

on was dry and warm. I stood on a large flat stone and watched him. My body was erect and pulsing like the sound of the waterfall falling into the pond, wave

after wave, as I stood with my arms along my sides. The moment came and left

me spent, with the greatest feeling of satisfaction and joy that I had ever known.

I loved my grandfather so much and I knew he loved me even more, if it were

even possible.

"Benjamin. You have entered another dimension. The feelings you just

experienced are the reasons why you are here."

"I am happy we came to this place grandfather. Thank you."

"The third dimension is a wonderful place. It is full of joy and love...."

"But why is there so much misery?" I asked.

"Hear me Benjamin. I will tell you when I am finished."

I hung my head and stood in silence. I cannot ever recall Grandfather

scolding me.

"It is like I said Benjamin. There is no answer as to why. In this dimension

we are the beings of what you would call circumstance. Some say it is cause

and effect. It is the duality of our existence which most people cannot

understand. For many, who do not know how to reason and think clearly, they become the problem they cannot solve. No amount of reasoning will answer

why until you find it inside yourself like you did a few moments ago.

Two parallel lines can meet in infinity. A minus times a minus, equals a plus.

Governments have kept the applications of higher mathematics hidden

from the masses, barely educating school children as to the correct equations.

Now I know this is beyond your grasp as a twelve year old. You simply need to

get the idea. Speaking of twelve Benjamin, I would like to wish you a Happy

Birthday. This is my gift to you."

He took a paper from his pocket and handed it to me.

"These are the two volumes of Buckminster Fuller's writings published by

the McGraw Hill Company in the 1960's. The United States Government

confiscated all of the volumes of these works from the libraries. NASA has the

only remaining copies, except for you.

"The books are in your room at the farm." He smiled and I hugged him.

"These volumes will help you understand the fourth dimension. Keep

them to yourself and share them with those you trust. Oh, and there is one

other present."

Grandfather handed me a Swiss Army Knife. "Your mother said you could have it. Took a lot of talking but she gave in. Promise me you will use it wisely?"

"I Promise."

That was many years ago for me.

Today I am fourteen. Twelve seemed like it was so long ago. That year did not change my mind about math though the books are still with me.

That evening after devouring the goulash, and following dinner, it was my habit to turn on Television. Instead, returning to my room where the books were spread on the floor, my mind kept wondering why they ended up in my backpack. There was a connection with the Victorian book, as it had the floor plans of the house I lived in. How he knew about the 'Catcher in the Rye', puzzled me until I moved on to the Calculus book. The lettering on the cover read: 'Dimensional Calculus-The Language of Space Travel.'

Handling all of this information at the same time was too much. Nobody but mom knew about my Star Trips and the Astronomy nights at my window. Mom did not know about the Astronomy Map Log for it had my own personal thoughts inside. Reading them was not for her. She was religious, going to

Mass every Sunday to the point of seeing that my education included the Catechism of the Church meaning my attendance in parochial school.

Sunday mass and communion required one of my most dreaded experiences; confession.

Confession was a sacrament of the church that was just another thing to do if you are a Catholic. It was not a problem until I was fourteen when my real sins began. These were sins that started two years ago. I had no idea that I was such a sinner until last week when I entered the confessional.

Father Edward

"Bless me Father for I have sinned."

The priest was not an old man. It was his first parish where he taught us and played basketball with us while working as a priest.

"What are your sins?" He asked me.

Before confession my list was memorized. My list of sins was not too short as I didn't want to seem like a saint.

"Father, I disobeyed my mother."

"How did you do this?"

Hoping he wouldn't ask me what it was, my story had to be invented in the booth. "I did not clean up my room Father."

"What did you do instead my son?"

Whenever he called me son my teeth came together almost grinding. "I went out and played basketball Father."

"What are your other sins?" He asked me.

"I pushed a boy in school. He fell on the ground."

"Why?"

"He fell because I pushed him Father."

"I meant, why did you push him"

"He got his brother in trouble." It was getting uncomfortable in the small confessional.

"Is there anything else you wish to confess?"

Glad that he didn't ask what the brother did, I told him, "No Father."

"You have attended mass and taken communion each week?"

"Yes Father."

"Do you do anything to yourself or have bad thoughts?"

"I don't think so father."

"Do you play with yourself?"

"Sometimes, but most of the time I play with my friends."

"That's not exactly what I meant Benjamin."

"Then what do you mean Father?" I asked knowing what he meant.

"Do you play with your sex organs and masturbate?"

"No Father." I lied, surprised at how quickly my answer came.

"Do four Our Fathers and three Hail Mary's. Let us say the Act of Contrition, together."

Since the confession there is a question about whether the act Father mentioned was a sin. This is serious, for if it is a sin it is one being committed almost every day, sometimes more.

Sometimes it happens at night when my body explodes during sleep. Someone must be able to answer this question.

It was then that Holdon Caulfield came into my life. I took <u>Catcher in the Rye</u> to bed with me.

CHAPTER FIVE

Mother gets the Message

My wake- up call came at 7 am, half an hour earlier than usual. I am not a morning person so it was hard for me to wake up as I walked into the bathroom to drain my dragon. This is an expression I learned from one of my uncles when they took me to hunting camp. Waiting for the dragon to get soft sometimes took a few minutes. Removing my boxers and T Shirt I wished my showers were in the morning instead of at night. Mom let me wear my shorts and shirt to bed on my thirteenth birthday. She must have decided that it was less expensive than buying pajamas. During my thirteenth year I grew a few inches. At the moment my hand held some of those inches and finally the water rained into the toilet.

My bathrobe was hanging on the back of the door. Mom would not let me go to the other rooms in the house in my underwear. She said she wouldn't do it so neither should I be allowed. Calling me for breakfast, which would be oatmeal, toast and eggs, I followed my nose and stomach down to the kitchen where mom was pouring a cup of coffee. She still wouldn't let me drink coffee.

It was the caffeine she said, not knowing how much caffeine was in the soda I

drank.

"What is this police card doing on the counter?" She asked. Mom sat

across from me as I concentrated on spreading jelly.

"He was talking to Mrs. Fontana when I came home yesterday."

"Did you do anything?" Mom did not know about Officer Sherwood.

"What did he want?"

"He wanted to know where you were.

"What did you tell him?"

He asked me questions that were stupid so he wants you to talk to him.

Call him after noontime. Mrs. Fontana can tell you. Mom, are you in trouble?

Did you do something wrong?"

"Oh Benjamin," Mom cried, "They think you are being neglected because

you are here alone. That is why Mrs. Fontana is looking out for you."

"Don't worry mom. There isn't anything they can pin on us. We look out

after each other, right?"

"What is this policeman like? Do you know him?"

"He is not a nice man. He looks evil mom. If he comes here don't let him in the house."

"You get ready for school. I will clean up the dishes." Mom sighed. Cleaning up was usually my job. She was looking very tired and sad which did not happen often. There must be a way to fix this problem. Another one of Grandfathers sayings entered my head.

"There is a solution to every problem Benjamin otherwise it would not be a problem.

The secret is to find the best and right solution."

"Is that true for math?" I asked him.

"Right solution is the human one. Math has a correct solution. You will learn the difference if you master math. With humans no matter what we know there is the X factor."

"X?"

"It will come to you Benjamin. Of that I am certain."

"When Grandfather?"

"One day it happens like a bolt of lightning. You will reach a point of high achievement. What you have done with your young life so far is a wonderful thing. You have taken steps with your study of Astronomy, placing you above the ordinary. Standing where you are now Benjamin you have joined the universe of ideas. You play in the ordinary world yet you have stepped above it. Someone will come into your life like a bolt of electricity. You will know it when it happens."

The only part that made any real sense to me about what Grandfather said is the bolt of lightning.

From that day on Math was one of my new languages.

Mother talks to Officer Sherwood

Instead of calling him, Mom went down to the police station to meet Officer Sherwood. When she arrived Sherwood was on patrol, which meant he was in the donut shop hitting on the waitress. Josh told me that one.

Finally waiting for him in the station for almost an hour, she was shown into the interview room. Officer Sherwood entered and sat across from her.

"Sorry to keep you waiting Ms. Winslow."

"What is this all about?" she asked showing him his card.

Officer Sherwood took out a notebook and a pen that he placed on the table. "Well you see Ms., your son seems to be spending a lot of time alone. A neighbor called us to say he stays home at night while you are working."

"What neighbor?"

"We can't tell you that."

"Can't or won't? If someone is talking to you about me you need to tell me who that person is."

"We can't tell you because we have to protect the identity of the person. Won't cause we don't have to."

"Then officer this conversation has ended." Mom stood up to leave.

Officer Sherwood picked up his pen and tapped on the table. "What I really wanted to talk to you about Ms. is the man your boy is meeting."

Mom told me how she turned and looked into Sherwood's eyes.

Grounded Again

Mom always left for work before school was out. Today she was waiting for me as I parked my bike in the garage. She was going over the tools on the workbench.

"Hi mom, what are you doing here?" I greeted her.

"Benjamin. Officer Sherwood told me you had something to do with a false alarm yesterday. We talked about a lot of things, especially about you."

"Officer Sherwood is a jerk!"

"What about the false alarm? It was from Mrs. Fontana's phone. How did you do that?" She picked up a box that held my electronic tools. Pulling my phone set with the clips from the box she looked at me with a strange smile.

"You used this didn't you?"

"Mom, he was harassing me and Mrs. Fontana."

"No. No. Don't answer me. I know what you are capable of Benjamin."

She told me about her meeting with Officer Sherwood. "He is more than a jerk. He is a dangerous jerk. Tell me about the man in the bookstore Benjamin."

Up until this moment in the garage, my lies to mom were few, like "I don't know", when I knew. Yesterday my answer to her question would not have been the same one given to her today.

"What do you want to know?" I asked.

"How long have you been going to the bookstore?"

"Yesterday was my first time." Explaining to her about the ticket in the jar, at the bazaar, and how it led to me going to the bookstore yesterday. Mom put my phone set back into the box and picked up her purse.

"After talking to Officer Sherwood I went to the store and talked to him. He told me how disappointed you were not winning the dictionary. He said you spent a long time looking at the books on the shelves and how he let you use the phone to call me so you wouldn't be late checking in. Then I went across the street to the Hair Saloon asking Darleen about the man across the street."

Darleen cuts my hair and works on Mom every Saturday. "Why?" I asked.

"To find out if what Officer Sherwood told me was true. He said the man likes young boys. Darleen told me the man in the store was not a strange person that he likes to help others, especially boys who have no place else to go after school."

"Josh's brother Mikey works there on Saturdays Mom. If there was anything weird about the bookstore he would have told me. Darleen is right. He does help Mikey. If anyone is weird it's Sherwood Mom."

"I know that now. Darleen told me all the things Officer Sherwood does. He is always after women doing some shady things when he stops them in their cars."

"What kind of things Mom?" I promised Jason that his secret with the cop and his mother was safe with me.

"Never mind that now Benjamin, I have to get to work. You are grounded for two days for pulling that false alarm trick."

"Mom, he was harassing us." Telling her about him sitting in the patrol car outside our house didn't make any difference.

"Call me by six Benjamin. There is a pizza in the freezer and a tuna casserole for dinner."

Starting to protest was not going to work. She was late as it was. At least she didn't find out about the books. Or did she? When my punishment was over the first thing to do was to go back to the bookstore. For now there was the mystery of the hidden room to solve.

CHAPTER SIX

Star Map Thirteen

We spent my thirteenth birthday in the grotto. As grandfather spoke I fell back on the moss covered stones and closed my eyes.

"The first dimension Benjamin is like being on a railroad track. We can go forward or back talking only to the person ahead of us or behind us. If I tell the person ahead of me that the sky is blue or tell the person behind me the sky is black, they will send the information along the one dimension track. You will never know what is said at the end of the line. The message is never received as it was sent.

The second dimension adds movement to our left and right. In this dimension we can run back and forth along the side of the track communicating with the first dimension creatures. A train is an example of traveling in the first dimension and ships on the water would be an example of a second dimension moving on one plane in any direction.

In the third dimension we are able to travel forward, backward, left and right and then up and down like an airplane in the sky or submarine in the water.

First dimension creatures are not able to see second dimension creatures as the second dimension creatures do not see those in the third dimension.

Now Benjamin, I am going to show you how to travel in the fourth dimension. You will be in the third dimension but you will enter the fourth dimension by being in the same place at the same time. In order to do this you will violate both the law of gravity, and the law of impenetrable force and in entering the fourth dimension you will be invisible to third dimension creatures. You know what the law of gravity is, how it works, and what happens if you break it.

The law of impenetrable force states 'that no two objects can occupy the same space at the same time.' You know, Benjamin, what will happen if you break these third dimension laws."

"How do we find the next dimension, the fourth dimension, Grandfather?"

"It is found at the end of time. For example Benjamin the dimension for speed is length divided by time."

Sitting up from my comfortable place I opened my eyes and saw Grandfather walking on the log next to me.

"If the future always exists, Grandfather, then there is no end of time."

"That is clever Benjamin but your reasoning is unsound. In ancient Greece they would call you a Sophist. Look at it this way. Time is a continuum. When time goes from one dimension to the next it ends in the old dimension and begins in the new dimension. Man writes a new book at the beginning of each new dimension."

"Like the bible?"

"Exactly, in order for anything to exist in the third dimension it has to have duality, such as hot and cold, black and white, before and after, high and low, something and nothing."

"Don't forget male and female." I added.

Grandfather laughed. "Yes Benjamin. You are learning. The forces of reason and logic are mathematical. A higher calculus in the fourth dimension alters the elements of reason in the third dimension. We cannot apply our current calculus to discover an ultimate existence in the fourth dimension. It takes dimensional calculus to do that."

"So Grandfather, there is a fifth dimension too?"

"Yes."

"I do not understand the dimensional calculus texts you gave me as hard as I try."

"You will Benjamin, in time, when you find the secret room. The reason you need to know all of this, centers on discovering the secret room."

"The bolt of lightning that you told me about will be in the secret room?"

In the grotto when Grandfather mentioned the room, I could not bring myself to ask him what the room was or where it could be found. It was up to me. He walked out of the cave past the falling water. We came to a logging road. Following him, we climbed the trail along the creek bed. Tons of water cascaded over the rocks pouring into deep clear pools. Reaching the trail above the falls, he stopped and pointed to a building on the mountain. Looking at the round dome like shape I knew it was the observatory where his friend lived.

"We call him 'The Mountain Man'. He watches the sky, looking for smoke from fire in the daytime and he observes the stars and heavens at night."

As we entered a gate to his garden, The Mountain Man greeted us. On his hilltop farm he grew many plants and flowers. Dinner was ready as we walked inside his cabin. We ate fish from the creek and the vegetables out of his garden. They were the best. Mountain Man poured me a small glass of his wine. He called me a young skunk for drinking it so fast.

After dinner, as we were sitting on the porch watching the sunset the Mountain Man went inside and returned with a box.

"Here is a gift for you Benjamin, Happy Birthday." Opening the box I found a beautifully bound Guide Book to sky watching.

"The Perseids meteor showers happen tonight. You are invited to stay and watch them. They will be here around 3 am and the sky is crystal clear like the water in the creek."

Around nine o'clock they sent me to bed while they continued to talk and drink.

"Wake you up around two." They told me.

That morning in the very early hours the Mountain Man took me to heaven. My map will show you where we were standing on the top of the mountain. The meteor shower was the beginning of my education in the search for God. The priests had it all wrong, or at least the Mountain Man convinced me about where God was living.

My Father's Secret

We finally came down from the observatory dome as the eastern sky

glowed in the first rays of dawn. Venus sat above the horizon looking like a

bright star. Reflecting the sun, a satellite flew along the same path as the moon,

and settled below the surface of the earth.

Lights from the meteors reminded me of the streaks of golden arrows

leading Peter Pan and the Darling Children to the island of Never Land, one of

the books Grandfather sent to me when I was seven years old.

Those were ancient times for Benjamin.

Spending the night on the mountain was a night where many of my

dreams turned from the earth to include the universes beyond.

Grandfather left me alone with the Mountain Man that night, returning as

we sat down to breakfast. Before my grandfather found us in the garden I asked

the mountain man if he knew my father. "Yes Benjamin. He broke a few laws.

His crimes were against his own self."

"What did he do that was wrong?" He was the first person who would talk

about my father. Later it became obvious why Grandfather left me alone with this man. One of the reasons was to answer questions about my father, answers that Grandfather and my mother would not give to me.

"He abused both you and your mother."

"Abused?"

"Yes Benjamin. Your father was a very heavy drinker."

"How did he hurt us?"

"He spent everything on drinking. There was never enough money for food. Then he broke the law of nature. While driving drunk he hit and killed a little girl."

"Did he stop drinking after that?"

"Yes. He did."

"Then why didn't mom and grandfather forgive him for his wrong? That is what we are taught in Catechism."

"Who can forgive what some men do?" Neither priest, nor judge, nor governor can undo the harm one person inflicts upon another. Kill, rape, rob, injure, destroy or abuse? Nature has the absolute sentence. The individual lives with the worst punishment for what your father did."

"Why won't they forgive him? Why won't he come to visit me?"

"You are old enough to know now Benjamin. Soon you will be a young man.

"Grandfather and I think you have a right to know about your father."

"Then you are going to tell me what my father did?"

The Mountain Man hung his head and put his hands together.

"Benjamin. The girl he killed was your sister, his own little girl."

"I had a sister?"

"She was a beautiful child. Forgive him Benjamin. We cannot."

"My Father was Grandfather's son?"

"Yes."

"I don't understand."

"You will. Your father left you when you were very young. He started drinking again until no one could reach him."

"Shouldn't I love my father?"

"We still love him. We just can't forgive him when he took off to live with a bottle of Ripple."

"Then I can forgive him!"

"You have nothing to forgive him for."

"For…I don't know. Not seeing me since I was seven years old?"

"You can do that." He picked me up like a leaf on a log then, with a hug lifted me over his head.

"We all have to grow up Benjamin, in spite of our parents, no matter how much they love us and we love them. When you come back next year I want to see your Map Book."

God is Found Hiding

On the way back to the farm Grandfather did not ask me anything. Everything he told me about the dimensions was confusing. Though the mountain man answered my questions, there were still a million more to come.

When we scrambled through the undergrowth into the forest, Grandfather led me into a stand of tall pines. The tops of the trees were far above us. The sun did not reach the floor of this dark and quiet place. We walked upon the soft needle and moss floor brushing against the ferns.

"It is nice here Grandfather. This is a nice place."

"Yes Benjamin," he said, "These tall and massive trees will be carried away soon on the backs of the log trucks."

"What will they become Grandfather?"

"These trees will become tall poles carrying the wires of God Benjamin."

"God, Grandfather? What do you mean?"

It was another one of his deep and heavy thoughts, as Josh would say when I told him.

"Electricity Benjamin, God is electricity."

This was going to be hard to explain to Josh.

"Electricity has all the attributes and requirements of God Benjamin. It is in everywhere.

It is in all places at all times, in the cell of a rock to the cells of an unborn child. Electricity is omnipotent. There is not one cell in the universe where electricity does not exist. It is a forgiving God for all who believe in it. Since man has discovered electricity, he has found the secret of himself. There is no power greater than electricity. Man has used the resources of earth to produce God. The electronics of our world propel his existence. Electricity does not laugh at man. Unlike the leaders of the Churches, electricity does not ask for belief in the God that it is. The Popes, the Bishops, and Priests laugh at their own God.

Electricity was the God creating both heaven and earth. All of the creatures in the waters and upon the land were generated by this God. All things whatsoever came into being and exist as a result of this God.

"Father Edward would flip if he heard this Grandfather."

Benjamin, the world was created in a dimension we know nothing about.

"How do we find that dimension Grandfather?"

"It is easy. We avoid those who think and believe otherwise, Benjamin like that priest of yours."

"What about my priest Grandfather?"

"Humor him. Benjamin. Humor him."

"Mom isn't going to like this."

"Just watch your Priest's hands Benjamin."

"Father Edward is Holy man of God Grandfather."

"When they inducted the Arch Bishop of Boston Benjamin, the Bishops hoods were the hoods of a clan."

"They are men of God Grandfather."

"Yes Benjamin. They are men with hormones who want what every man wants, what the French call 'The Little Death'.

"What is that grandfather?"

"It follows the God of Priapism which you have come to experience every day.

You mean the 'Morning Glory'?"

"Even the holy men of God cannot escape the God of Priapism Benjamin."

"Why does mom believe in them?"

"She is trying to keep you from going to hell Benjamin."

"Then why is she putting me through hell to do it?"

"She believes in you but not herself."

"What about you Grandfather?"

"Me? I am just one of those trees, in this forest, carrying the wires of God Benjamin."

"What about the Mountain Man?"

"Come here on your next birthday Benjamin. Take good care of your mother.

You can do this best by taking care of your friends. Your mother is a friend. Josh and Mikey are friends. Many will claim to be a friend but will deny being a friend at the first sign of trouble."

"What about the room Grandfather?"

"Benjamin. Stop being a couch potato. Work out. Be tough. Be yourself. When you find the room you will know about the dimensions."

He did not answer my question about the Mountain Man. He left me to figure out what the secret room was all about. My thirteenth birthday was the beginning of a new life, sending me in search of a room, another way of looking at God, and what could be done with a mother and a priest who had other plans for Benjamin.

My salvation was Josh with the help of his brother Mikey.

CHAPTER SEVEN

Jason helps me find the room. He discovers my Map Log.

Mom left for work backing out of the driveway as Mrs. Fontana came outside.

"Benjamin these are for you. Are you OK?" She handed me a container of molasses cookies. "That officer came by this morning to ask me if you used my phone yesterday. I told him you didn't and I don't think he believed me. Is he giving you a hard time?"

"No ma'am but he is bothering mom."

"Do you want some advice Benjamin, just a little bit?" She didn't wait for my answer.

"We live in a police state. Don't do anything to make them mad at you even if they are wrong, especially if they are wrong."

"Yes ma'am." Thanking her for the cookies, she went inside as my dark thoughts went with me up the stairs to my room. There can't be anything better than cold milk and her molasses cookies. Having been grounded with her cookies helped me forget my troubled day.

Josh called. He wanted to ride down to the river and throw stones. When he found out my mom grounded me he asked if he could come over. Mom, who was at work by the time Josh called, said he could come over for an hour but only if we did our math together. She knew Josh got straight A's in math so it wasn't hard to get her permission.

We didn't have any math homework. When Josh came over, he had some of the cookies and we went to my room. His eyes lit up when he saw the Dimensional Calculus book. "Where did you get this?"

Telling him the story from the bazaar to why mom grounded me, Josh smiled.

"You know how much I like math Benjamin.

Nobody can know. They would call me a freak in school.

"Mikey thinks I'm a freak but he's my brother."

The next hour was one of the best ever. Josh read some of the thoughts written in my Map Log. We went through the floor plans of the Victorian book, when I told him about my search for the secret room. We went up to the attic searching for a door or some way into the room. Finally after an hour we came down into my room. Josh went over the floor plans again.

Discouraged he suggested we smoke. We went into the bathroom closing

the door and turned on the ceiling fan. We sat in the bathtub facing each other,

neither one of us speaking. Josh leaned back putting his head on the edge of

the tub.

"That's it!" he cried. "Benjamin the hidden room is above us." Josh stood

up pointing to the ceiling above the shower. "All we had to do was turn the plans

upside down and over."

Following his finger, pointed toward the ceiling, I saw what he was talking

about. We flushed our butts down the toilet.

The house was built before indoor plumbing. When the bathroom was

installed the owner at the time, choose a large closet next to my room. The door

to my room off of the upstairs hall was located three feet from the wall. The

bathroom was on the other side of this wall. Inside the bathroom, the wall was

three feet less than the space from the corner to my room. Josh saw this sitting

in the tub.

"The door leading to the room above us has got to be in your room!" Josh

smacked his fist into his other hand. "Yes!"

We stood in front of the wall inside my room. "All this time we thought the bathroom was on the other side of this wall." I told him.

"Lot of good it does." He said. "How do we get inside the wall?"

"We could tear out the wall." I suggested.

"Sure Ben. Freak out your mom. The room wouldn't be a secret then. You need more hiding space Ben. You're getting all these books. Think of all the things we could keep in it."

"Things we could do in it."

"In the house plans it shows a flat roof in the center with a round dome like thing." Josh said. "That's got to be it."

"It's called a cupola!" Benjamin told him. "Josh. How are we going to get in?"

"The answer has to be in the book Ben. What did the librarian tell us about how to find things in a book?"

"It's called the index or the table of contents."

"At least you pay attention to her during library class Ben."

"If you and Mikey didn't keep trying to figure out how to sabotage her globe you might learn something too Josh."

"Every time we have library she brings that globe over to our table for her geography test."

"Miss Agnes says we can't get enough geography. She loves her globe more than the books."

"Mikey says she goes to bed with it."

Josh picked up the Architecture book. "Here! You go through it. I'm going to have a look at this calculus book. Why do you suppose Mikey's boss gave these to you?"

"When Friday comes we can find out. Go with me?"

"Sure, we can go right after school." Josh agreed.

Josh had to leave by six.

"Let me know when you find the section on moving walls." He bounced down the stairs, hopped on his bike leaving me alone with my casserole. After calling mom who wished me a good night, it was time to take a shower.

Being preoccupied with the mystery of how to get into the hidden room, my hand accidentally turned the shower handle to the left. It was a right turn all the other times. There was no telling why I turned it the wrong way tonight. The sound coming from the other side of the wall made the hair on my neck stand

up. Someone was in my room.

CHAPTER EIGHT

Josh and Mikey Spend the Night

Mikey was just about as cool as anyone in school. His father was in

prison. Eric, his mom's latest boyfriend, slept in the living room on the couch

where Mikey copped most of his cigarettes. Josh hung out with me after school

and kept to himself at home. My mom tried to keep Josh from spending time

with me while she worked, especially at night.

Asking her why, "Why can't he spend the night with me?" She replied,

"Josh comes from a bad home life."

"Then that's all the more reason for him to stay here," Hoping my reason

was going to talk her into it.

"Benjamin. Sometimes you have to accept my decisions without asking

for a good reason. Or any reason, because working at night makes it hard on

me to look after you. Mrs. Fontana looks out after you at night. I can't ask her

to be responsible for another boy."

My head was thinking only of myself for it almost opened my mouth to ask

a question, one that would have hurt my mom and caused her deep pain. At the

time of pleading with her, the information the Mountain man gave me about my father was still to come. The question stayed inside me. *"What if you had*

another son or daughter Mom?"

Benjamin Decides

"It is time for me to look out after myself." He thought.

Taking the towel in one hand, then going to the phone downstairs, he

called them. It was only a few minutes before Josh and Mikey rang the doorbell.

While waiting for them it seemed like a good idea to turn off the lights

downstairs, especially the porch light. Josh and Mikey would put their bikes

around back in the garage and not make any noise to disturb Mrs. Fontana.

They would make sure no one saw them from the street especially any cruising

police cars.

In going downstairs first, to call Josh, you could say going into my room

was not the first choice, something not to be done alone. For another reason,

which can't be explained, my hand reached into the shower and turned the

handle to the right. Not seeing the wall slide but hearing the sound of it closing

would allow Josh to begin where this all started. Next, Josh was too streetwise

to believe in magic. Watching his mother and her boyfriends on the living room

rug, since he was four years old, allowed him to figure out that magic was not

Santa Clause, the tooth fairy or Mr. Stork dropping his brother down the

chimney. Mystery to Josh was his father living within twenty miles from him and

never sending a birthday card. Mystery to Benjamin was Josh understanding

calculus in the seventh grade.

Going downstairs butt naked was not a choice really. My excitement

showed but, like my nude body, there was no one to show it to. As soon as they

rang the bell, Josh and Mikey walked into the darkness where the mystery

began.

Josh spoke first. "Ben you found something."

Mikey walked toward the stairs. "Ben. Put something on will you?"

"I will when we go to my room, Mikey. I was in the shower when it

happened."

"What? When what happened you dork?" Mikey asked.

"Cool it Mikey!" Josh told his brother. "He doesn't know anything about

this Ben."

"Then why is he here?"

"We got grounded outside. We can't go back until midnight." Mikey said.

"Wish I could stay out that late." I told them.

"Not three or four nights a week you wouldn't with no place else to go.

"Nothing is open in this town after 10 O'clock."

"You could have called me."

"Yeah sure Ben, then your mom would have called the police. We don't want another foster home where you have to fight for a place to sleep.

"How did you know I was naked Mikey? It's dark in here."

"Your dick glows in the dark Ben. Besides I spend a lot of time in the dark. You learn to see more in the dark when you spend as much time in it as we do.

"This is news to me Josh." Benjamin said.

"We don't tell you everything Ben. If your mom finds out we hide outside at night she will tell someone else. Word gets around in this town." Josh said.

"You are keeping secrets from me Josh.?" Ben asked.

"One slip and we get taken away Ben. We don't have a Dad looking over our shoulders. If they took us away from our Mom we would be in deep dip....."

"Shit!" Mikey finished.

"You don't have to swear." Josh cautioned. Besides you can't see in the dark Mikey."

"No but I could tell Ben was naked by how excited you are Josh."

"If Ben is right about the entrance to the secret room we can spend the night here."

"Sorry guys. You and Josh have your own secrets. I don't have to be here."

Mikey was twelve years old but in many ways he was more mature than both Josh and Benjamin

"Well you sure are welcome tonight Mikey, especially if you can keep a great secret."

"Is it OK to smoke in here?"

"No way, maybe on the way home." Josh told him.

"Later. It's always later isn't it? Wait until you grow up. Grow up or throw up!"

"Screw you." His brother told him.

"There isn't any of you who can you that to me." Mikey laughed.

"You are my best friends but we have a mystery to solve here tonight. We can duke this out on the playground tomorrow if you guys want to but we have to make it through the night." Mikey told them.

Mikey worked his way over to the couch and plopped down on the cushions.

"You two can go upstairs and die for all I care. I'll stay here until your mother comes home from work and kicks me out. What do I have to do with this mystery of yours?"

"Mikey. You work in the bookstore where this mystery started. The man you work for gave us the books to solve it. You are part of this whole thing whatever it is."

"What if I don't want to be?"

Josh walked behind the couch. "There is an exhaust fan in the bathroom. You can smoke in there."

"Then let's get going and solve this bookstore mystery."

"It's more than that Mikey." Benjamin said.

"Jesus Josh. What if mom smells the smoke?"

"That is one of the problems with smoking Ben. Your mom smokes. Do you think a smoker smells a smoker?"

Sitting next to Mikey on the couch, my hand slipped around his shoulder. He put his head next to mine, then standing up said, "Let's get the hell upstairs Ben so you can get some clothes on."

They entered the bathroom. Mikey sat on the toilet and lit a cigarette.

Josh turned on the ceiling fan. "

Explain this to us." Josh asked Ben.

"Wait." Josh went into the bedroom with me. The books were on the floor where we left them earlier. My boxers were on the bed. "Do you think Mikey will let me wear just these without thinking 'faggot'"?

"Mikey always thought wearing clothes protected him from the boyfriends."

"Your mom's boyfriends came after you guys?"

"Nothing protects you from the boyfriends Ben. You just take what they have to give you and hope for better things."

"What about your father Josh? Did he know?" Benjamin asked.

"Once, my aunt who lives in North Carolina explained it to me. She told me my dad loved the bottle more than anyone, more than me, that maybe someday he would maybe even be sorry."

"You think he will?"

"My grandmother told me someday I would be old enough to ask him."

Josh cried. "How old will I have to be Ben to ask my father about sorry? I put my arm around Mikey so many times and said, Sorry."

"We have to bring Mikey into our secret room then."

"What secret room Benjamin?"

"Turn the shower faucet to the left Josh. Then we will see."

CHAPTER NINE

My Bolt of Friendship

With my boxers on Jason followed me into the bathroom where Mikey was sitting in the tub with his feet on the edge, smoking a menthol cigarette. Josh sat on the toilet lid.

"Before we start this we have to swear that no one but us will know what we are doing."

"Your mom will know Ben. She will have it figured out before you suck in your first spoonful of raisin bran." Josh said.

"Yeah but she won't know about the room if none of us say anything."

"So how are you going to explain us here when she gets home?" Mikey asked.

"If we find the room you both can hide in it."

Josh stood up and reached for the faucet handle. "If the room is above us then we can climb through a window and go home without her knowing."

"What if the room doesn't have a window?" Mikey asked as he blew a cloud of smoke toward the ceiling fan.

"Which way did you say this turns Ben?"

"No. Wait!"

"How long do we wait Ben? When we start shaving?" Mikey asked.

Pulling Josh's hand away from the faucet my heart jumped as the question came to me.

"We are friends, right?"

Josh put his hand on my shoulder. "Remember what we said about friends Ben?"

Mikey rolled his eyes. "You two are nuts!"

"A friend is anyone who will die for you."

"Giving yourself to a friend is the best thing you can do."

"Not only nuts, but faggots!"

Josh pushed his brother's feet into the tub. "You are one my best friends Mikey. If it came to that I would die for you to keep you safe.

Mikey threw his cigarette butt into the sink. "It's only a secret room. Nobody dies here."

Josh left the bathroom. He returned with the Architect Book. "We aren't talking about dying here. We are talking about friendship. Secrets, secrets found from the bookstore. The man in the bookstore is part of this and you work in the bookstore Mikey. Benjamin and I have not told you about his grandfather,

the telescope and the Maps. Can you keep all these things between just you

Benjamin and me? Ben and I think the room is an answer to help us get away

from here."

"Mikey. Check it out. If you stick with us on this we will help you do the

Great Library Globe affair."

"You mean it Benjamin?"

"She won't know what happened. Your plan will go down in history."

"It will take a crane to lift her globe from the table." Josh laughed.

"This will make school a special learning place." Mikey said.

"Turn the handle of that faucet Josh. Benjamin's mom won't be home for

three hours."

Josh turned the handle to the left. The sound was enough to send them

walking slowly from the bathroom to Benjamin's room.

CHAPTER TEN

The North Star

Benjamin led them into his room.

"Whoa!" Mikey cried.

"What is that opening in the wall?" Josh asked.

"That," Benjamin said, "is the way up to the secret room."

Josh looked into the opening. "There are stairs here guys. Now what do we do?"

Benjamin sat down on the bed. He looked at the books on the floor. "You have the book that shows the floor plans Josh. How far up do the stairs go?"

Mikey picked up the calculus manual. "What does co-sign mean? Why are these books here? This one looks like one in the bookstore. Is that where it came from Ben?"

"I'm afraid so. Yeah. Look Mickey you work with this man. How did these books end up in my back pack the other day when all I did was try to find out about winning a dictionary?"

"It beats the hell out of me Ben."

"What do you do in that bookstore?" Ben asked.

"I move piles of books. They come into the place every day. He has me move them from the first floor to the second floor to another room filled with other books."

"What does he say to you?"

"What do you mean?"

"Is he like weird or strange?"

"You could say he is both." Mikey told them. "He is like a grandfather or at least what I picture a grandfather is. Like Josh and me don't have a grandfather. We have fathers but they are not around when we want them to be, and who knows maybe like our mom says, it is a good thing they aren't."

"We don't know if she is right Ben. All we get is her stupid boyfriends and one of them is only three years older than me."

Ben sighed and closed the book he was holding. "My mom doesn't have boyfriends, at least not any that she tells me about. All the men I know are uncles who take me hunting and fishing sometimes when they feel like it or when mom makes them do it."

"But my dad is in prison." Mikey said.

"And my dad is in Las Vegas." Ben said. "Doing what we don't know."

"My dad is only a few miles from here. He is right down the street for Christ's sake, compared to your father's, who are locked up or far away. My dad is right down the street man!"

Josh cried. He tried to hide his tears in Ben's pillow. "My mother won't let me see him. My grandmother won't take me to him. When I call her she keeps saying I should wait until I am older."

"Why Josh. Why do you have to be older than you are now?"

"What does your grandfather tell you Ben? Why doesn't your father want to see you?"

"He killed my sister. He was drunk driving in a car."

"Is that why your mom doesn't want you seeing him?"

"She doesn't know I know."

"Was it your grandfather who told you Ben?"

"No he didn't. It was the wild Mountain Man who told me."

"You know a wild Mountain Man?" Mikey asked.

"A friend of my Grandfather's who lives on top of the Cascade Mountains in Oregon."

"He was in the bookstore last week." Mikey said.

"We have to go back to the store." Ben told them. "Maybe even now like right now."

Benjamin started dressing pulling on his pants and sliding his T-Shirt over his head.

"The store is closed. It's dark out. What about the curfew?" Josh asked as he lifted his head from the pillow. Officer Sherwood would love to find us breaking into the bookstore at this hour."

"OK. Let's figure this out now." Benjamin told them. "There are things we don't know about all of this, things which we need to know before going any further."

"Like what?" Mickey asked. "Can we go into the bathroom for another cigarette?" he asked. "Besides, I have a key to the bookstore."

Ben looked at the open space in the wall. "Sure. Sure why not? The stairs can wait. You both need to know a lot of things and we need to know who this Bookstore Man is."

"I say we go up the stairs now." Josh said.

"A cigarette comes first!" Mikey cried.

Benjamin put his arm around Josh. "OK both of you. Since we are in this together and found the secret room which has something to do with the bookstore where Mikey works, then we have to be in this, all for one and one for all."

"We can be the three mice!" Mikey shouted.

"We didn't know you could read Mikey." Josh said.

"Sometimes the books opened up Josh and the words just jumped up at me, you dork!"

"Look! Josh. Mikey. From now on we have to all stick together. If my grandfather is right something is going to happen which will change our lives."

"I say we go up the stairs to the secret room." Josh said.

"This mouse votes for a cigarette first." Mikey told them.

"Close the door to the secret room and head for the bookstore now." Ben added.

"Cigarette!"

"Room!"

"Bookstore!"

"Nothing like all of us being together on this." Benjamin laughed. He tied his shoe laces.

"We have to be very quiet when we leave the garage."

"Who died and made you the boss Ben?" Josh asked.

"It takes 50 earth years for the light from the North Star to reach earth Josh. Mikey can have his smoke on the way to the book store. The room will be there tomorrow, but the Mountain Man may not be."

"Then we must vote on this Benjamin. Visit the secret room or the Mountain Man first. Which is it Ben?"

Josh walked into the bathroom. He turned the shower handle to the right. The wall softly closed in Ben's room.

"Who knows Ben? The Mountain Man could be my dad."

As they rode through the park to the bookstore Josh smiled. Imagine a wild Mountain Man being his father. Mikey blew the smoke from his cigarette into the wind. Benjamin decided to tell them about the books above his closet. Was grandfather a wild Mountain Man?

What the three of the friends didn't know, as they entered the side door of the bookstore, is what wonderful adventures waited ahead.

Ms. Agnes in the library had no idea what was about to happen to her precious globe, the one she used to convince her pupils from the three grades, three times a week, that the world was a safe and wonderful place.

Mikey pushed the side door open. Josh and Benjamin followed him into the darkness.

Benjamin felt the presence of the Mountain Man before he saw him in the store.

"Is that you Grandfather?"

"No Benjamin Grandfather is waiting for you in the room above us. Have you discovered the room he told you about?"

"We think so."

"You mean these two friends are in on this with you?"

"We decided to stay together, Josh, Mikey and me."

"You didn't go into the room?"

"We came here first."

"What do you three want to do, now that you are in this together?"

"Maybe go to school tomorrow and help Mikey with Ms. Agnes's globe?"

"And then?"

"Go into the room together."

"Benjamin. You will all go into the fourth dimension. Do they want that? Do you know what will happen? You must tell them about the next dimension."

"What if we want to leave the room once we get there? Can we come back here and not go back into it again?"

"When you enter the secret room you will be able to go wherever you wish.

"Mom's sure not going to like this." Ben said.

What about Josh and Mikey? "Can we come back here?"

"Yes."

"I knew we needed to come here first! Where is my grandfather?"

"He is upstairs waiting for you."

"Then when grandfather talks to me we will solve this problem of what to do?"

"In time, yes Benjamin."

"Will Josh and Mikey be here, when grandfather and I finish talking about the room.?"

"Benjamin. Neither your Grandfather nor I have ever failed to keep you in touch with your friends. They have to decide to go into the room with you. They can leave you if they want to and do whatever they want to do with the rest of their lives. It is up to them."

"Then where is my grandfather now?"

"He is waiting in the room."

"You mean the secret room above my bedroom?"

"No Benjamin, the room above us. Mikey and Josh can wait here."

"Maybe they can go home now. It is after midnight."

"Look outside of the bookstore windows Benjamin."

Officer Sherwood was pacing up and down the sidewalk.

"What is he doing here?" Benjamin asked.

"He followed the three of you over from your house Benjamin."

"He is a faggot!" Mikey said.

"We can't let him catch us on the street." Josh told him. "Let Benjamin get this over with."

Benjamin walked to the stairs wishing this could be the stairs to the secret room. Whatever he decided, he wanted it to be over with before his mother returned from work. Whatever he decided, his mother would take everything

from there. Then it was her problem. Benjamin realized his mother was hiding

the truth. At least she was shielding him from the real world of Benjamin,

especially about who his father and grandfather really were.

While Josh and Mikey waited in the bookstore Benjamin climbed the stairs

where that night, he learned about the N-Dimension and Quantum Computer.

CHAPTER ELEVEN

The Anmagnascope

Benjamin followed the Bookstore Man up the back stairs walking between stacks of books, which almost reached to the top of the stairwell. He entered a small room where his grandfather sat rocking in a large chair.

"Grandfather!"

"Hello Benjamin."

"Remember what we talked about in the grotto about the fourth dimension Grandfather?"

Benjamin walked over to the chair and reached for his grandfather.

"You are not here are you, at least not in this dimension?"

"The Mountain Man, the Bookstore Man and your Grandfather, we are in the fourth dimension. You know where the room is now, don't you Benjamin?"

"Yes grandfather. Jason and his brother Mikey helped me. "They are down stairs with the Mountain Man."

"Let us hope they don't try to touch him like you tried to touch me."

"Jason knows about the fourth dimension. Mikey would freak out."

"What about you Benjamin? Are you willing to try it?"

"After all the talks we had in the Grotto and on the Farm, it is time for me to do it. That is why we came here first. We know where the room is. It was my decision to come to the bookstore figuring that the information on getting to the room came from here."

"If you go to the fourth dimension your mother and teachers and friends won't be able to see you Benjamin. Do you want that?"

"I can see you and you're in it."

"Once you enter the next dimension, you will learn how to let others see you but not until you have mastered the time travel between dimensions. There are guides and ancient rules to follow in order to keep you a safe traveler. Both you and Jason need to learn the dimensional calculus. You have the books hidden in your room?"

"Yes Grandfather. The three from this bookstore are hidden as well, in case mom came home early."

"Here is the first guide for you. In the third dimension, time is kept by *astronomical clocks,* which are regulated to keep sidereal time. The hours of the clock are easily reduced to degrees. The astronomer always reckons the hours of the day consecutively up to twenty four."

"What if we are in the fourth dimension Grandfather?"

"Then you are in a parallel universe where time is measured by quantum laws. If you and Josh want to learn, then it will be necessary for both of you to spend time in the room digesting the works of Buckminster Fuller. Unlike time in the third dimension you will learn about space and time in the fourth dimension."

"What will mom say when we disappear and she can't see us?"

"Oh, you won't be gone that long, though she will wonder what you are doing up in your bedroom."

"But she doesn't approve of Josh."

"Mothers mean well. She has to let you select your own friends as long as they don't hurt you. Josh excels in math and you need all the help you can get. I think we can arrange an hour or two each night while she is working."

"How will we ever learn dimensional calculus in a couple of hours each day?"

"That is an interesting question Benjamin. When you are in the secret room, there are no astronomical clocks. The telescope in your bedroom may measure the ascensions and declensions of the stars but the Anmagnascope in the secret room deals with quite another set of stars not found in this dimension."

"You mean the third dimension."

Benjamin sat down in the rocking chair. "You don't mind if I sit on your fourth dimension lap do you grandfather?"

"Of course not you rascal! How many times did you fall asleep on my third dimension lap before your mother took you away?"

"What will it be like when we are in the fourth dimension together?"

"It's never happened Benjamin. We'll have to try it sometime."

"Very funny, Grandfather."

"Speaking of which, it is almost time for your mother to return from work and you are not even home in your bed. Go down and get your friends. Tell them they can return to their place. You hurry home."

"What will we do about Mikey? Is he going into the room with us?"

"No Benjamin. Mikey has other things to do to help us. He will be the keeper of the gate post, guarding the four corners of the universe, while you and Josh get ready to travel."

"He knows about the room."

"Take him there. He should find the room interesting."

"Then we should go to school tomorrow morning?"

"Tomorrow is library science day Benjamin.

Ms. Agnes has the fifth grade and the sixth grade students for three hours. The three of you have the global plan ready? Josh, Mikey and you can't disappoint the rest of the students."

"That's right, the bags of sand. This secret room business made me forget."

"Friday, after school, you and Josh come here and the Bookman will give you more instructions about the room. Two hours studying in the secret room with Quantum Computer is equivalent to spending sixty earth days in the third dimension."

"How is that possible?"

"You and Josh are about to find out."

"When Mikey finishes with Ms. Agnes's globe we may all be grounded or in jail."

Benjamin stood up and turned around. Grandfather was gone. Going downstairs he found Josh and Mikey in the back room. Mikey was drawing a scene on the computer from the paint program.

"Better erase that!" his brother said. "Remember Zero Tolerance?"

The screen showed a naked policeman being run over by a truck. Above the scene Mikey wrote; SHERWOOD IS A FAGGOT!

"We can put this on the police car tonight." Mikey told them."

"We have to get out of here." Josh told them.

"You want Zero?" Mikey jumped up and deleted the program. "Zero is him doing our mom!"

Josh walked to the window. The clock in the park struck 12 AM. "So where did everybody go Ben?"

"They left us to figure things out. Here's the plan for tomorrow. We can go home now. Sherwood is finished with his shift by now but driving around looking for us. Tomorrow we go to school."

"What about the room?" Josh asked.

"We come back here after school. Then we go to my place and go up to the room. We all go together so it means none of us see the room until then."

As they were riding their bikes home Mikey slammed on his brakes. "Today is GLOBE DAY!" he cried.

Josh did a slide and stopped in front of his brother. "How could we forget? Everyone will be there with the sand. THE HOURGLASS SHOW presenting Ms. Agnes and her humongous globe!"

"Ms. Agnes and her humongous globe," They sang together. The police cruiser came down the street.

They all took off into the park leaving Officer Sherwood to guess where they would come out. Josh and Mikey went into the trees and headed north to their place. Benjamin went across the field toward home hoping he could make it before Sherwood drove around the block. As he entered the garage, Benjamin knew his friends got home unnoticed. The police car stopped in front of his house as Benjamin locked the front door. . As he turned the bolt on the door, his mom greeted him. How was he to know that her car was in the driveway, that she came home early? He came in the back way to the garage.

CHAPTER TWELVE

Project Globe

Benjamin opened his jacket and threw it against the wall of the sacrosanct. The priest was due at any moment. His mother was not going to allow Benjamin any excuses for being outside the house at night.

His only escape was to serve as altar boy during the Friday morning mass. This absolved him in the eyes of God for disobedience to her. She was the mother who looked over her son as God looked over His Son.

Benjamin wondered if Officer Sherwood attended the 6 AM mass at St. Vincent Holy Church. If so, maybe the body of Christ would choke him to death in front of the altar.

Josh served with Benjamin and Father Edward that morning.

Benjamin slipped out of his robe waiting for Josh in the hall next to the sacrosanct room. He lifted his school bag and started walking out of the door leading to the school building behind the church sanctuary. Josh probably went to the bathroom.

Father Edward stepped in front of Benjamin.

"Peace Benjamin."

Benjamin stopped walking and looked up. "Father, good mass."

"You handled yourself very well son."

Benjamin cringed.

Your mother wants me to meet with you after school today Benjamin."

"She does? Why father?"

"She just wants to make sure son that you are in good hands."

Mikey suddenly came through the front door behind Father Edward. He pointed to his shoe. It meant the game was afoot. Mikey loved reading Sherlock Holmes.

"Sure Father, in the rectory after the last class?"

"We can meet in my office Benjamin?"

"Yes father."

The Globe

On Fridays following lunch period, Ms. Agnes taught a geography class in the library. All of the students in the fifth grade and the two classes in the sixth grade attended. They were required to know the locations of all the countries in the world and on which continent they were found. "Someday you may wish to go where these people are." She told them.

Ms. Agnes had this very large globe, which sat on a heavy brass stand. It turned slowly in each direction but Ms. Agnes instructed her students to turn it only from left to right. "This is how the earth turns, children." She smiled.

The globe had a diameter of 48 inches. Josh thought it weighed at least 25 pounds, being almost as tall as many of the students. The continents, islands, and landmasses were clearly marked along with the oceans separating them. Longitudinal and latitudinal lines were drawn in black. "The equator and the Greenwich meridian were darker than the other lines." She told them for the 100th time.

One basic problem with Ms. Agnes's globe was its age. Countries, which no longer existed, since the First World War, were still listed on the globe. Ms. Agnes insisted, when the students brought it to her attention, that all answers on the tests were to be taken directly from this globe. Every Friday afternoon she struggled with the large globe. She carried it from the corner table in the library to the center of the room, where her students sat in a circle waiting for the Science of Geography lessons to begin. "Geography is an exact Science." She told them. "If we don't know where we are on the planet Earth, how will we ever be able to reach the stars?"

It never mattered that Edo was no longer the capital of Japan or that Siam was now Thailand. The globe could not be wrong.

Josh had failed many of her tests. Benjamin gave the wrong answers and passed.

"It is called the Ms. Agnes' test of who can 'Beat the Global War on Suck!" Mikey told them. "Benjamin. That globe has got to go!"

Mikey was the one who figured out how to end the war.

"What war?" Josh asked.

"It's like quick sand." Mikey told them.

"Like yeah. What does quick sand do?"

"It can suck you down man."

Mikey's plan required the cooperation of all the Library Science students. Those who were afraid to take part in it did not have to bring a bag of sand to the library or at the very least stay home the day of the game, or they could just keep their mouths shut.

No matter what happened, when the game was over, the school principal was sure to use the new zero tolerance rule.

If a student pushed someone they were suspended for violence. None of them knew what would happen if they were caught bringing the sandwich bags filled with sand, into the school. The picture of Ms. Agnes trying to lift the globe at the end of the geography class seemed worth the risk they were taking.

As it turned out, the pouring of sand into the Globe was an unforgivable act of terror against Ms. Agnes. If no one ratted on Mikey then no one would be punished. Mikey knew from the beginning that if his plan worked someone was going to pay for what they were about to do to the globe.

Not certain how the principal would handle this, he was willing to take the punishment. What they could do to him was nothing compared to how wonderful he would feel when the sand was in place.

As she carried the large globe to where her students waited, they put their backpacks on the floor. The sphere loomed above the students as it had each Friday throughout the years of her geography lessons. She passed the test questions to each student.

"You have 30 minutes to answer these." She instructed. "Anyone who fails to answer 90% of the questions correctly will have to take this course next week, and every week for the rest of the year until they pass. I will be over at my desk and there will be no cheating. You will all be allowed to turn the globe

for the answers. Ready? Start now."

Mikey pulled the drill from his backpack. Shadowed and covered by the

other students, he opened a hole into the top of the globe. Josh pretended to

study Alaska while keeping the drilled circle from falling inside. Each student in

turn walked over to the sphere with the bags and poured the sand, they had

carried into the library, down the funnel, which Benjamin held.

One by one they filled Ms. Agnes's Globe up to the equator.

CHAPTER THIRTEEN

Coming of Age

Mom didn't say anything at first.

She sat in the kitchen waiting for me to say something. Considering all the things happening during the day, a day almost over, around midnight, it seemed to me she should be the first to speak. What could anyone say?"

Well she answered that question. "You were out with Josh weren't you?"

"I was with Josh and and Mikey."

"Were you at their house?"

"No mom. Officer Sherwood was in their house so you know we wouldn't all be there."

"No I don't know! Seems like there are a lot of things I don't know about what's going on around here."

"That makes two of us."

"Benjamin, you have never lied to me, at least not that I know of. For years you have been someone living with me, my own son, who does all these things and reads all these things. Now you go out at night when it is against the rules. You spend so much time with the telescope your grandfather sent you.

Maybe I shouldn't let you spend a month in the summer with him anymore. How far do I have to go to shield you from harm?"

"Mom, I'm fourteen. Remember? You can't build a bubble around me. It's my world too."

"Benjamin. How can you talk to me like this? You are still a boy. There is so much you need to know."

"Like what mom?"

"All of the bad things that can happen to you, the hurt and the pain. You have to know how to handle them."

"Josh and Mikey seem to be handling all of them Mom."

"Go to bed Benjamin. Tomorrow you will see Father Edward. He can explain it to you better than anyone."

Global Friday

The bell rang ending Ms. Agnes's geography class. The students were fortunate in that she would not allow any of them to help her carry the globe back to the library table. The bad news was that school was over for the day. Only those students who would see the sinking of the globe were the ones given detention.

Mikey was one of them. He was caught in the Boy's Room during lunch without a pass. Part of his game plan was detention after school. Detention was held in the Library. Josh was in the principal's office, having been summoned from the library at the end of geography class.

He had no idea why he was pulled so quickly from Ms. Agnes's class. When he arrived in the office the secretary told him to sit on the student bench. Students called the bench the 'Docket'. Mikey named it following the showing of the musical <u>Oliver</u> in the school gym last year.

Josh was expelled for six months after the showing of "Oliver."

When the movie ended the students stood up from where they were sitting on the floor. Mikey started shouting "MORE!" Suddenly all of the students from the first grade to the sixth chanted "More, more!"

From the stage, Mr. Crispin, the principal shouted for quiet and order. The students quieted and waited for their principal to dismiss them. Unfortunately he took the time to call their actions a deplorable example of riot behavior. He advised them they were in danger of never seeing another movie in school. He told them that civil disobedience was not being taught in his school.

Mikey looked at Josh and Benjamin. They began singing, "Oh you got to pick a pocket or two Boys, you got to pick a pocket or two!" Joined by the other students they marched around the gym singing, "You've got to pick a pocket or two boys, you've got to pick a pocket or two!"

The students started to put their hands in their pockets, pulling out what they had in them, waiving their report cards, they had been given before the movie, throwing them in the air and dancing on top of them as they landed on the floor.

Josh then went to the back of the stage and took off all his clothes. He walked up behind Mr. Crispin and raised his hands before the assembly. Suddenly there was silence. The principal raised his hands also. He tapped on the microphone. Mr. Crispin had no idea a student was standing behind him, nude and smiling.

"Now that's more like it students. Please pick up your report cards and return to your homerooms." He felt strange as the assembly in the gym looked, not at him, but past him. Josh walked up to the microphone and said, "You know, you sandbaggers, you can't pick a naked man's pockets."

The students laughed and roared.

Josh was expelled for six months and he served that time in a juvenile rehabilitation center. When he was released and permitted to return to school he walked into the library smiling. The counselors were sure Josh would never know the meaning of civil disobedience again.

No more movies were ever shown in the school gym again.

The day it happened the students were directed out of the gym. As they were sent into the school's parking lot, Benjamin looked at Mikey. "That was something you would do Mikey, not Josh!"

"My brother is finally getting it Ben."

"Getting what? I don't understand."

"What a true genius he is Ben."

That was last year. Benjamin left the school building and walked toward the church. As he passed the school office he saw Josh sitting on the Docket bench. Officer Sherwood was talking to the principal behind a glass partition. Benjamin thought the officer was there to discuss the next DARE program. DARE always meant an hour with Officer Sherwood or Officer Mitchell in the gym. When the program started it took a year for students to figure out that they were expected to turn their own mothers and fathers into the police if the

students suspected or knew of drugs in their homes.

The program gave the officers a lever to seduce single mothers who

smoked marijuana instead of arresting them. Once word got around in the

classrooms, DARE was as boring for the officers as it was for the students.

Benjamin's mother was right. It was a bad world out there.

Benjamin headed for Father Edward's room. It was called an office but

the Priest lived in the room with his desk along the side of his bed. Benjamin

laughed at his thought about the world out here. What about the world in the

secret room? Was it any better? With these thoughts he knocked on the

Father's door.

CHAPTER FOURTEEN

Sacrament of Penance

"Come in Benjamin."

Opening the door to the room Benjamin was surprised to see the priest sitting in a stuffed chair between the desk and the bed. "Forgive me Benjamin. I was not ready for you."

Father Edward was dressed in boxers and a T-Shirt, with his bare feet spread out toward the door. "Excuse me and I will get a robe on. Please close the door."

Benjamin walked into the room and sat down by the desk. This was his mother's idea. Father Edward stood up. "If you don't mind Benjamin this is how I dress when I am in my room."

If Father Edwards only knew how I dress or don't dress when I'm in my room. "So don't put on a robe. What did you want to see me about Father?"

"Ah yes. Your mother called me this morning before mass. A bit early but then she works the night shift does she not?"

"Yes father. She does."

"Your mother worries about you son." Benjamin cringed. "You seem to be going against her will." The priest sat on the bed closer to him.

"Maybe you should put on that robe Father."

"Well we shall see. Those boys you hang out with. Are they true friends? Jason and Mikey?"

"Yes they are father."

"Josh has told me you two are very close."

"He told you that father?"

"Well not in so many words but I could tell he likes you."

"So?"

"Your mother said you and his brother were out with Josh last night when you were supposed to be home in bed."

"We were at the bookstore Father talking to my grandfather."

"Does your mother know this?"

"No father she does not know what we did last night."

"Can you tell me? It will stay between us boys."

"What boys' Father?"

"Well you boys and me."

"Oh. Yeah well no, Father. What happened last night is between Josh, Mikey, my grandfather and me?"

The priest reached over and put his hand on Benjamin's thigh. "You are all that close to each other Benjamin?"

A tent appeared in the priest's shorts. Benjamin looked at the rising pole in Father Edward's pants, then, lifting his head to look into the eyes of the man, Benjamin spoke softly. "Josh told me you were like this father."

"So I am Benjamin. So I am, but my needs are the same as yours."

"Maybe when you were my age father but yours needs have nothing to do with me, not now. Were you going to absolve me for disobeying my mother, questioning the church, not believing in God? Sure, we all jerk off, but you Father are a real jerk off to think you can touch my dick. Do you still have the scars where Josh bit you on your cock Father? You had him sent to McClaren Boys Home for six months! Fuck you and your god Father! You wanted to see him naked? Well he took his clothes off after the movie Father so you could see him. Did you jerk off in bed that night as they took him away Father?"

"That's not true Benjamin. None of what you said is true!"

"You sure fooled my mom. She even had you over for dinner on Sundays. Look here Father. Mom isn't running my life anymore. You sure aren't going to get any of us, Josh, Mikey or me into your confessional booth or your pants."

The priest stood up and went behind his desk. Clasping his hands together he sat down.

"Benjamin, you realize how much trouble the church can make for someone like you and your mother?"

"Sure Father. The church has been doing it for centuries. The village cops do it every day."

"That is heresy my son."

"I am not your son Father. Fuck you and the son of your God Father!"

"More heresy, the Holy Father will send you to hell Benjamin. You know that don't you, having been taught the catechism?"

"Father if there is a hell you better take a lot of ice cubes with you."

"Josh and I saw <u>Week End at Bernie's</u>, both the first and the second movie. The Pope, wherever he travels today, looks like the corpse in those movies."

"You will be brought before the church council!" Father Edward cried.

"Heresy Father?"

"The church and I only deal in the facts and the truth!"

"Does the Pope know you fuck little boys' Father?"

"Tomorrow both you and your friends will be expelled from the school. We cannot have this anti-Christ in our parish."

Benjamin stood up and walked to the door of the Priest's room. Opening the door, Benjamin turned to face Father Edwards.

"You realize Father today is Friday the 13th?"

"Get out! Get out! Get out!" the Priest cried.

Benjamin, before he closed the door of the Priest's room smiled and said, "Your hard on seems to be history Father."

As he closed the door Benjamin heard the priest crying. Walking back to the school entrance Benjamin waited for the students to leave the main door. Entering the office he saw Josh. Principal Crispin stood over him, and Officer Sherwood certainly wasn't talking about the DARE program.

CHAPTER FIFTEEN

One Beautiful Paradigm

Benjamin hurried to his locker. He passed the library windows along the hallway. Josh and Mikey were supposed to meet him later at home to discuss the secret room but there was a lot more to talk about today.

Detention would be over for Mikey at 4 o'clock unless Ms. Agnes discovered the new weight of her globe. Benjamin hoped Mikey would get away before she tried to move it back to its place on the library table, as if anyone could move it without a forklift.

As for Josh and his visit to the principal's office with Sherwood standing in front of him, as he leaned on the desk with his hands, there was no doubt that his friend was in trouble. Both boys had to be at the bookstore for instructions about the secret room. Right now, it looked to Benjamin that all of them would be grounded tomorrow.

Benjamin put his bike in the garage. Mrs. Fontana greeted him at her back door. "These are for you," she said, handing him a zip bag of freshly baked cookies. "You can share them with your friends."

"Thank you!" He said smiling. "Josh's mom isn't into baking much."

"I know how it is with young mothers today. They work so hard. Does Josh's mother have to work at night?"

"Ah yes she does." He wanted to say she tested mattresses, but knew it would not float if Mrs. Fontana asked him to explain. "She's a waitress at the diner."

She begged him to enjoy the cookies as Benjamin ran up the back stairs. Entering the kitchen he found a note from his mom on the table. It instructed him to call as soon as he got home from meeting Father Edwards.

When she got on the phone he was pleased to hear her voice. "Did you see him?" she asked.

"Yes mom. We talked."

Did anything happen? Were you able to turn on the tape recorder in your pocket?"

"He touched me mom but nothing happened. Everything we said is on the tape."

"Put it in a safe place Benjamin. Stay inside tonight. We'll talk about it in the morning."

"Goodnight mom."

"Goodnight Benjamin. Remember. Stay inside."

"Yes mom."

Benjamin ran up the stairs to his room and sat on the bed. Looking at the wall hiding the opening to the secret room, he thought of going into the bathroom and turning the handle to the left but soon gave up the idea, wondering what he would do when the wall opened. He reached above the closet and took down The Catcher in the Rye." Benjamin stripped to his underwear. Plopping down, he turned on the light above his bed leaning with some pillows against the headboard to read.

The next thing he knew his mother was pulling him onto the bed and covering him with a blanket. When she turned off the light and left his room he looked at his watch and saw that it was past midnight. Benjamin fell into a deep dreamless sleep.

There was nothing he could do now about anything. His last thought was that maybe Friday never happened. All of his muscles floated away along with his mind, along with any thoughts of keeping others safe from falling from the fields of rye.

The paradigm that the sun always rises startled him from his sleep as Josh and Mikey rushed toward his arms.

Breakfast with Mom

His mother brushed the hair from his eyes. "You have 15 minutes to get down for breakfast." She said."

Benjamin sat up propping himself with his arms behind him. "What about a shower? No shower last night."

"Just wash your face and brush your teeth. I let you sleep late."

He kept looking at the shower handle as he washed and dressed in the bathroom.

His mother set the plate of pancakes and sausages in front of him. She stroked his hair and sat across the table. "I heard the tape Benjamin."

"How did you find it?"

"You told me in your sleep. You talk in your sleep you know."

"Better not keep anything from you then, huh Mom? You listen to me while I'm asleep?"

"Well I heard a lot of things which didn't make sense."

"Like what?"

"That you saw your grandfather yesterday and someone called Mountain Man, lots and lots of nonsense."

"What kind of nonsense? Like what?"

"Things like star maps, secret places, calculus, which you don't take in school, and Benjamin, what is this about a globe with sand."

"That sounds really weird mom."

Benjamin was always able to talk while he was eating. If he needed time to think of an answer he would stuff food into his mouth and chew. No one can talk with their mouth full or at least try not to. It gave him time to think before he answered. She never thought he was trying to get more time to think about the answer.

"You were right about Father Edwards. I'm so sorry to force you on this man."

"Josh said Father Edward uses his collar to have sex with boys and takes communion with the devil."

"What does Father Edward do?"

"Yeah, like the devil made him do it so he can be forgiven.

Josh told the Parish Priest when he was twelve years old that Father Edward

was after him for sex."

"Twelve!"

"He even told the Sisters in school."

"What did they do?"

"Remember the time they sent Josh away to a boy's detention center for

six months?"

"Josh hit Father Edwards in the mouth and hurt him." His mom replied.

"Sure mom. Josh hit him real good but not in the mouth."

Maybe I don't want to hear this!"

"Nobody ever does mom. Josh told me if his own father weren't such a

drunk the priest would be gone, maybe."

"What do you mean maybe?"

"Mikey's father is in prison for the same thing Father Edward does to us

boys. Mikey is allowed to see Father Edward but he can't visit his own father in

jail."

Benjamin's mother went to the cupboard and pulled out the small tape player. "What if I gave this tape to Officer Sherwood? Would you boys be safe from the Father then?"

"Josh said you could tell the mayor of the village and the chief of police and the court judge. If you give the tape to Officer Sherwood, or any of them, it will never be seen again by anyone."

"How does Josh know so much? What makes him so smart Benjamin? He is a fourteen year old boy the same age as you?"

"We protect our mothers just like they try to protect us."

"He spent six months in a detention home mom. Josh was sent there when Father Edwards convinced the judge he needed counseling. Officer Sherwood told the judge he was a real trouble maker, and Father Edwards testified that Josh attacked him for no reason."

"What about Josh's mother?" Didn't she stand up for him?"

"You might as well grow up mom. Welcome to the real world. Josh's mom is having sex with Officer Sherwood so he won't take Josh and Mikey away from her.

"This isn't happening Benjamin. The world is not like this. Is it?"

"MOM!" Nothing will ever happen to make you ashamed of me. Things are going to happen to all of us, all good things, but you no longer run my life mom."

"Benjamin. Benjamin. Benjamin!"

"I've told you the truth mother."

"What are we going to do about this tape? What are we going to do about Father Edwards?"

"Josh will help me figure it out. Grandfather is here to help us. We may disappear for a couple of days, so don't worry."

"Disappear!"

"Take my word for it mom. We won't be far away. Mikey will keep you in touch with us. I Promise."

"This is your grandfather's idea then? Where is he now?"

"With him it's hard to tell mom. You know him. He comes and he goes."

"When I sent you to the West Coast each summer to spend a month with him I thought he would teach you enough to want you to go to college."

"He sure taught me a lot mom."

"Did he tell you about your father and what your father did to us?"

"No mom. The Mountain Man told me."

"So what you said in your sleep was not all nonsense?"

"I was trying to be a Catcher in the Rye mom."

"Father Edwards is meeting me in the rectory this morning after I drop you off at school. I don't know what a Catcher in the Rye is Benjamin."

"Mom, you have been one for years. When you talk to the priest you will know what a catcher is."

"You must come home after school. You know I don't have to go to work tonight."

"Make a deal with you mom. We are going to the bookstore after school to talk to the Bookman. Let Josh and Mikey come home for dinner with me, and we will explain what is going on about grandfather."

"I'll fix goulash Benjamin, your favorite?"

"Is it a deal mom?"

"Yes Benjamin, we have a deal."

CHAPTER SIXTEEN

Catcher in the Rye

Benjamin's mother was no longer nervous when meeting a priest. As a cradle Catholic, her education taught her obeisance and strict adherence to the cannons of the church. Our Fathers and Hail Mary's were the answer to all sins. The tape Benjamin recorded was the end of all Papal supremacy over Benjamin's mother. The archbishops and bishops protected their pedophile priests as they moved them to other parishes.

Father Edward welcomed her into the rectory office. She was glad not to be in his private room or cell, whatever they called it. It was the usual desk between cleric and church member, between lawyer and client or principal and student. The desk was always the wall placed between two people, one of them on the power side while the other waited to be seated on the weak side.

Humpty Dumpy could fall either way depending on who was pushing whom.

"Please have a seat." Father Edward told her.

"Thank you Father."

The priest closed the door to the office. He moved behind the chair where Benjamin's mother sat. He removed a large volume and placed the tome on the desk between them.

"This is a book on child psychology. It is titled, <u>Your Child Belongs to God</u>. Have you ever read it?" He asked her.

"No Father, I have never seen a book that large."

"You must know that Benjamin, your son, is a very disturbed child. According to the researches in this book, he has an aggression obsessive complex against authority."

Benjamin's mother looked directly into the priest's eyes. "You know that Father from reading this book, whatever it is? Why do you say Benjamin is disturbed?"

"He confesses to masturbation. In looking for a father figure who he doesn't have at home, he makes up stories about what other men do to him. He does not live in the real world. His stories are fantasy."

"What stories Father?"

"He makes up things that happen to him. He also hangs out with other boys who help him make up these stories, these lies, which he will tell to anyone who will listen to him."

"Benjamin has never lied to me Father."

"No but he has not told you the truth about his abnormal sex habits. That is omission, an even greater fib, when he masturbates and keeps it from you."

"Then Father, he does not keep this from you so how can it be wrong? It does not seem like boys would go around telling their mothers they are doing this."

"True. To hide it from you is nevertheless a sin."

"So, Father, you are saying my son is not telling me the truth when he is not telling me the truth?"

"I don't understand." Father Edward said.

"You wouldn't, Father. The truth is a dangerous thing. It has to be surrounded by a whole troop of lies, according to you Father."

"I had not expected this heresy from you. Benjamin must have learned this from you." He said, showing anger.

"No Father, thank God, if there is a God, Benjamin learned all this from his grandfather."

"Enough!" Father Edward slammed the book closed.

Benjamin's mom stood up and walked to the door. "You talk of heresy. You talk of sin. Father you speak as though there is something wrong with my son, my beautiful child who is now a man. He told me all about you. At first, I did not believe him because of my faith in the church. He told me about you Father. Now I believe him not because he is my son, rather because you have lied to me about my son."

"As a member of the church, this Holy Church, there is nothing you can do to change what is going to happen to both you and Benjamin."

"Father, I am going into the nave and pray to the Virgin Mary. Then we shall see what is going to happen."

"All your prayers will be in vain mother of Benjamin. The Mother of Christ has greater power in her very eye, than you will ever have in your entire soul. This church has more power and influence than you will ever have in your heart!"

"Then you better hope your dick has a lot of influence with God Father."

Friday

Father Edward's faith was strong. He felt the Church was behind him as it had been since he was ordained. The boys he sexually abused were not sons of the church's elite, the district attorney, the sheriff or any of the church's council members. He was selective about the boys. They could cry all day and all night but no one would take them seriously.

Josh knew this. He told Benjamin the story of what happened when they sent him to jail. They called it a Youth Detention Center. It was a place where Father Edwards kept you when you were a sinner, and where the county administered their wards, children who were detained while their parents fought off drug addictions or domestic violence. He told the story of how Father Edwards was the priest who looked after the boys locked in the rooms of the detention center.

Father Edwards did not take Josh seriously, especially when he was returned from the Detention Center to his parochial school.

The Tape

On Monday morning Josh, Mikey and Benjamin walked into the hallway to their lockers. Ms. Agnes was not working today. Her doctor recommended she rest over the weekend, before looking into the problem she was having with her globe.

Benjamin handed the tape to Josh. Josh walked into the office where he was on detention. Mikey watched as his brother entered the principal's office.

"The docket is screwed!" Mikey said.

"Josh may end up in the same cell with us."

"The screws would never let that happen!"

"What are Screws?" Benjamin asked.

"They call them Correction Officers. Josh said they are on the bottom of the list in the justice system."

"What do they do that is so mean?"

"They pee in your soup if they don't like you Ben. They decide if we go into the cottages."

"What are the cottages?"

"The cottages are where the counselors take care of you."

"What kind of counselors Mikey?"

"People like Father Edward Ben."

"Isn't the juvenile center supposed to rehabilitate?"

"Josh says rehabilitate means to get you to agree they are right and you are wrong."

"What if you don't agree with them?"

"Then you are de-habilitated and sent to the camps."

"Like the Jews were sent to in World War II?"

"Worse. They call it boot camp but they only want you to see it their way."

"It doesn't make sense Mikey."

"Like the Bookman told me Ben. The mind can be a terrible thing."

The Roller Blades

"We better get the hell out of here before that tape is played on the PA system." Mikey said.

"Not really. We have two copies." Benjamin told him.

"If Josh can put it in the system and broadcast it over the school's announcements, we better be gone."

"Josh can do it Mikey! Then we can split and go to my place."

"You realize dude that the law will be all over us, the principal, the police and especially your priest friend."

"They can't get us at my place Mikey. They have to have a search warrant." Benjamin told him.

"What if they just break in and grab us. You know what the local judge is like. He will say he signed the warrant after they do it!"

"They can't do that Mikey."

"We can't let them do that Mikey."

"Welcome to the real world Benjamin."

"Then you tell me Mikey. How are we going to get to the bookstore from here?"

"Why do we have to go to the bookstore?"

"The room Mikey, we need some final instructions. Remember the room?"

"Josh said you two were going to disappear for a few days."

"We need to find out how to do it first."

"What about me?"

"You will be our go between."

"I will be the one who works the faucet in your bathroom to open the entrance to the secret room?" Mikey asked

"You really think I believe all that stuff, that fourth dimension and the other universes?"

"You don't have to Mikey. You just have to believe in us."

"You are two weird guys. One of you is my brother? No way can I help other people man."

"OK. OK! Mikey. Remember when the man in the bookstore got you a pair of roller blades?"

"He called me and said that he had a surprise for me, so what?"

"The Bookman gave you those skates."

"He promised me that if I moved a ton of books to the third floor of his building, he would have a surprise for me."

"You moved them without knowing what the surprise was?"

"He told me it was something I really wanted."

"Josh and I wondered where you were for three days."

"When he gave me the roller blades, he watched as I put them on and took off down the street."

"Your mother's friend thought you stole them from her son."

"We had the same size and some creep took his from his locker in school."

"The boy's mother called the bookman. He told her he bought them for you, that he had the receipt."

"So what does this have to do with me believing in you two weirdo's?"

"You mean the skates?"

"What did you do with them Mikey?"

"I took them over to the boy's locker in school and left them there. I Gave them to her son."

"Why? You knew they were your skates."

"His mom has cancer. She is dying."

"You don't want us to think your soft Mikey?"

"You both want me to be soft on you too?"

"If you can help a kid like him, then you can help us too."

"Can I see the room?"

"Sure. You have to work with the Quantum Computer to get us back here."

"It sounds like too much work for me Benjamin. Can't you jerks find someone, who even cares if you return from wherever it is you are going? What if Officer Sherman comes into your house and takes whatever you guys call it, Quantum Computer, away?"

"They can only do that Mikey if you allow them to enter the room."

"What can I do? If I help you then we are in the same boat together."

"No, Benjamin explained, we shall all be in the same Spaceship together. You are the gate keeper and you have a friend who will help all of us."

"Greg? How do you guys know about him?"

"You have a friend Mikey that you haven't told Josh and me about?" Benjamin told him.

"We promised not to tell anyone about us." Mikey said.

"Then don't. Josh says Greg knows more about computers than IBM."

"Then your mom in on this one Ben?"

"She agreed to let you come over every night."

"So I could let her in the room?"

"She can't know about the room Mikey!"

"What is in that room Ben?"

"We are going to find out tonight. Grandfather says you can go in the room but that one of us must stay here to work the door in order for us to get back here. You will get to see an Amagnascope whatever that is."

"Get back here from where?"

"From the next dimension Mikey, where this room will take us. Be a good skate for this won't you?"

"The Bookman is in on this Benjamin?"

"Yes."

"Then count me in." Mikey said.

CHAPTER SEVENTEEN

The Faculty Meeting

The sun was into Friday afternoon as Benjamin and Mikey found their way to the side door of the school. Father Edward was walking from the rear of the church as they exited into the parking lot.

"You two know this is an emergency exit only, don't you?"

Mikey grabbed Benjamin pulling him toward the cars behind the school building.

"This is an emergency exit Father."   He said, as they ran away from the priest.

"Both of you must stop, right now!" the priest cried.

"Sorry Father. We have something important to do."

Father Edward shook his head as they ran from him. "We will see about this later." He called after them, and entered the building. There was a meeting in the faculty room.

The meeting started as he sat down. He seated himself next to Principal Crispin across from the table where the other members of the faculty sat watching the Father.

"Father Edward. Glad you could make our meeting today. It seems we have some serious problems to discuss here." The principal told them.

"And I have some issues to bring up here Mr. Crispin. Two of them concern a student in your sixth grade class."

"Well we may as well get started on the first item here. As the principal of this school you are aware that discipline is my problem when it comes to the classroom."

All of the teachers around the table nodded their heads in agreement. Father Edward nodded also.

The principal continued. 'Number one, Ms. Agnes is home with a nervous condition. The globe she used in the library cannot be lifted or moved since her last class met yesterday. Next, a police officer is investigating the activities of two of our students. When Officer Sherwood came into my office to explain the problem, one of the students just happened to be with me at the time. His name and the name of the other student involved shall remain anonymous for the time being."

Mr. Crispin stood up when the secretary from his office interrupted the meeting.

"What is it?" He asked.

"I'm sorry Sir, but I am locked out of the office. My keys are in my purse, which is on my desk. There is a student in there and he won't unlock the door."

"What student? Why won't he unlock the door? How did you get locked out? Why won't he open the door?" Mr. Crispin was flustered.

"He locked me out sir when I went to the bathroom."

The principal turned around to face the other teachers. "We shall see about this! What is the name of the student?" He asked his secretary.

"Josh. It's Josh sir, the student on detention."

Father Edwards ran from the room. He rushed down the hallway and tried to open the door to the school office.

"Open this door now Josh or the wrath of God will fall on you." He shouted.

Helplessly the priest watched as Josh slid the tape into the school's public address system.

"You all know my voice." Josh spoke into the microphone. "My friends and I did not want to play this tape while the other students were in school. The other voice on the tape is that of Father Edward. He asked Benjamin to meet him in his room yesterday. It was Benjamin's mom's idea to put the recorder in

Ben's pocket. No one ever believed my brother and me when we told them the

things Father Edward did to us; not the Pastor of this church, the nuns, or

anyone, because Mikey and I were always in trouble with the police. Benjamin

believed us. Benjamin's mother believed him. Benjamin, Mikey and I hope you

will enjoy listening to the tape."

The faculty members listened. Mr. Crispin listened. All of the janitors in

the school heard the tape as it played over the school's speakers. Father

Edward listened as Josh smiled at him from the office windows. When the

recording ended Josh opened the door and walked past the priest.

Josh headed for the bookstore.

CHAPTER EIGHTEEN

Policemen Need Donuts

Officer Sherwood signed the duty roster at 3:30 PM on Friday afternoon.

The sergeant handed Sherwood the schedule list covering the shift activities.

The list included:

1. Finish all paperwork from the preceding shift.

2. Interview the mother of a boy named Benjamin Winslow, address

attached;

And the mother of boys named Jason and Mikey Singer, address

attached;

Determining connection with said boys to the owner of the bookstore,

which is located on the corner of Broad and Waverly streets.

3. Do not, under any circumstances, stop any cars in the village tonight.

4. Report to the chief at 1100 hours in the morning.

Officer Sherwood met his shift partner at the donut shop.

It was not a good time to go to the pawnshop, where he began working

most of his shifts. Reporting to the chief in the morning was not a good thing. It

usually meant a dressing down for his behavior as the night officer. On several

129

occasions the chief tried to fire him for his conduct and behavior while on duty.

He conducted routine patrol stops making unwelcome suggestions to women

who filed a complaint against Sherwood only to settle out of court. The village

insurance company paid for the damages claimed, thus Officer Sherwood

continued to serve and protect the village taxpayers.

Officer Sherwood was not a nice guy.

Jason enters the Bookstore

The store had books from floor to ceiling, wall to wall, upstairs and

downstairs. The side door to the store was unlocked. Jason entered and

walked to the back room of the store. Mikey called this room the cyberspace

warehouse. At this hour, the store was open to customers, but no one was

around. Jason walked along the stacks. If his brother and Benjamin were not in

the store, he was not certain what he would do, now that he played the tape.

Benjamin asked him to broadcast it to his teachers during the faculty meeting.

The bell on the front door stopped ringing. "They must be at the police

station." He said to himself.

In the cyber-space room he walked between the stacks. The cigarette

smoke gave Mikey away.

"So do we have a plan or what?" Josh said to the books on the shelf.

"What took you so long to get here Josh?"

Mikey sat on the floor behind the next shelf of books smoking a cigarette.

"Jesus Mikey, what are you doing here?"

"We were supposed to meet here before we went into the secret room. Remember?"

"Yes I do. "They almost grabbed me when I ran from the office. Father Edward tried to grab me by the neck but he got a kick in the crotch."

"Balls you say!"

"If he had two he would be king."

"Too bad he is a queen."

"Where is the Bookman?"

"Upstairs."

"Where is Benjamin?"

"He went home to get something, some book he had to have."

"Ben told you we were going up to room tonight?" Josh asked.

"Benjamin's mom is fixing us dinner. We are staying there tonight." Mikey told Josh.

"We have to go there tonight. Ben and I have to go somewhere for a few days."

"He told me that Josh. This thing about computers, quantum computers, dimensions and the crap about me being a gate-keeper, isn't real is it?"

"Yes it is Mikey." The Bookman said, walking into the room. "When Benjamin returns we will get started."

"That is if he returns." Josh said. "Officer Sherwood will be looking for all of us tonight after what we did to Father Edward."

"You mean he will be trying to get the tape?"

"No." Josh told him. "He will be after our mothers."

A voice called from the front of the store. "Hello. Hello!"

"That sounds like Officer Sherwood." The Bookman told them."

"Now what do we do?" Josh asked.

"Mikey will go talk to him."

"So what do I say to Sherwood?" Mikey asked the Bookman.

"Tell him we have lots of books here. Maybe he will buy one."

"You mean you want me to stall him? Sherwood only reads his paycheck."

"Yes, at least until Benjamin gets here."

"Sherwood has a partner sitting outside. How is Ben going to get inside the bookstore?

"There is an entrance on the roof. In the city many people come and go from the roof tops."

"Except Benjamin isn't a Batman. How does he get up there on your roof?" Josh asked.

"Remember when you were two years old Josh?"

Josh threw his hands in the air.

"You wanted to climb. All young children want to climb, from their mother's arms, from their cribs, from the playground to the trees. Men climb into their aircrafts, into their spaceships.

"The building has a ladder on the other side Josh. Mikey went to the front of the store. "This is too much." He told them.

"Josh." The Bookman said, "Benjamin has been climbing to the stars for many years."

"Benjamin and I will be climbing the stairs tonight, to the secret room."

"Does it frighten you?"

"Not if Benjamin is with me."

"Then you will meet Quantum in the secret room."

"Benjamin has the whole quantum theory in his closet. When you and Benjamin enter the fourth dimension, time is not the same like it is here. You will return from the secret room in the same place and at the same time. People here will not be able to see you when you walk back through the gate."

"Will we be able to return here later and be seen?"

"Yes you will be able to return.

Midnight Friday

Benjamin laughed when Josh told him about the playing of the tape on the schools PA system. Mikey said nothing.

"I am the one they will suspend! If they let me back in school it will be a miracle.
My lessons will take place above the police station for the rest of the school year!"

"Look at the good side Mikey," Josh told him, "They don't show up at the police station until ten o'clock in the morning."

Mikey sat at the table in Benjamin's kitchen.

"Now what do we do?" He asked.

Benjamin's mother put the food on the table.

"We enjoy dinner. I can't understand this." She told them. "Maybe when I wake up tomorrow we can figure out what to do and what's going on."

They all feasted and said goodnight to Benjamin's mom before heading upstairs to Benjamin's room.

"Sitting on the floor next to Benjamin's bed, not one of them wanted to start another adventure after what happened during the day.

"Now what are we going to do?" Mikey asked.

"You ask that question every morning." Josh said.

"So I am the gate keeper who opens the door to the secret room?"

"You asked for now what?" Benjamin said.

"Good going Mikey. You have the globe grounded. You pissed off Officer Sherwood tonight by asking him if he could read. Father Edward is crying in his room. Our bikes were on the other side of the bookstore. I don't know how they got there but we made it back here OK.

You can't go to school tomorrow because you got to go to the courtroom above the police station for your math and English lessons. You are public enemy number one in the eyes of the law." Josh told him.

"OK you nerds! This public enemy is going into the bathroom to fag one.

You want me to turn the shower handle to the left?"

There was a loud knock on the front door. Someone or some persons

were breaking into Benjamin's house.

Josh looked out of the window. "We have company!"

"Sherwood?" Mikey asked Josh.

"He brought his riot squad and three police cars."

Mikey jumped up. "See you guys. The gatekeeper has a job to do. Hope

you faggots make it back from that room upstairs."

"We'll be back before you know it Mikey. Save some cookies for us!"

Benjamin whispered.

"Not likely brother. When Sherwood finds me in the bathtub there will be

hell to pay. Better get in the bathroom before I forget which is my right or left."

CHAPTER NINETEEN

Bookman Explains Grandfather's Quantum Computer
Earlier That Same Day

Mikey returned to the cyberspace room. The bookman took him and Jason to the second floor. Benjamin greeted them as he was climbing down a ladder from the roof.

"Looks like we're all set," Benjamin said. "The book is right here."

"What did you say to Sherwood to get rid of him?" Josh asked his brother.

"He wanted to know where you and Benjamin were. Right now they are both heading for our house. Hope Eric's not home."

"If they don't find us Mickey he will be right back here." Josh said.

"The front door to the bookstore is locked. The side door is locked. Now what do we do?" Mikey asked.

Benjamin handed the book to the Bookman. "Our bikes are in the alley on the next street. We can get there from the roof."

"So how did our bikes end up in the alley Ben?" Mikey asked.

"Ask him." Benjamin pointed to the Bookman.

"The room is waiting for you, all of you. Here is what you can do to get away from all the events of the day. Benjamin will take this volume to the room where he and Josh will learn how to travel from here to the fourth dimension."

"Here?" Josh asked.

"Here is the third dimension, this time and this space. Follow the directions Benjamin that your Grandfather placed in the computer. Study this volume in the room. You will find that your Grandfather is waiting for you and Josh to learn the first N-Dimension formulas."

"My computer skills aren't that great." Benjamin confessed.

"Josh can help you find what you need to know Benjamin. He had plenty of time to learn his skills when Father Edward set him up in the Detention Center.

"What is important is the map information you have learned over the years. In order to navigate along a parallel dimension both of you will need to work together, Josh with his knowledge of calculus; you with your star maps, and both of you working with your Grandfather's quantum machine."

"We will learn how to operate the Anmagnascope?" Benjamin asked.

"Yes."

"And Buckminster Fuller's two volumes Grandfather gave me!"

"It is a new language, another universe for two young people to discover."
The Bookman told them.

"What about the third young person? Where do I fit in?" Mikey asked.

"You are the gate keeper of the secret room. The three of you have
known each other for over three years. Who better to guard both your brother
and Benjamin, than you Mikey as they learn how to travel into the next
dimension?"

"What if the police torture me and make me rat on them?"

The Bookman laughed. "You have been in this store for almost six
months. No one is going to torture you when you have a sanctuary in all these
books. They may make you do your lessons in the police station every morning
but they have to let you go when the teacher leaves."

"What if they don't? Officer Sherwood or the Judge or Father Edward can
send me to the Juvenile Center. Worse put me in the basement cell beneath the
police station. They won't even let you visit me."

"Mikey! If he can take your bikes from in front of Officer Mitchell who is waiting outside the bookstore then he can take you from any detention center or jail cell." Benjamin told him.

"What do I do about the room then?" Mikey asked.

"You make sure no one, not even Benjamin's mom, gets into that room."

"Look Bookman, this kid doesn't know much about math or quantum computers. It seems that if someone got into the room there wouldn't be anything there for them to see because everything there would be in the fourth dimension?"

"You would be a great police detective Mikey." Josh said.

"No way, thank you. So answer my question!"

"You will see when you enter the room tonight Mikey. Trust us." Benjamin told him.

The Bookman handed the Buckminster volume to Benjamin. "Read the pages marked and we will meet here in three days. The reason the room must be guarded by you Mikey is simple. These computers in the secret room are being sought after by men who will use them for evil and criminal purposes. It is hard to understand now. Later you will know why. To reach the fourth dimension in a parallel universe the quantum computer has to be placed in your dimension. If this computer fell into the wrong hands of say, the federal government, or some politician or priest, our project would be compromised. They would find all of us at the farm before we moved the Sunflower's parts to the moon."

"Benjamin and Josh might never return to this dimension if you gave away the secret of the room." The Bookman told him.

"Maybe they don't want to. What's been so great about being in this dimension?"

We have a lot to learn. From now on you are our hope. Take good care of all of us."

"We have to go now." Benjamin said. "Sherwood will be after all of us. My house is next."

"Keeper of the gate, Mickey smiled. "I kind of like that!"

"Your first major test is close gatekeeper." The Bookman said.

"We will make sure you have enough cigarettes Mikey." Benjamin promised.

"There isn't any smoking in your house Ben."

"The gate keeper has his own bathroom now with an exhaust fan. The gatekeeper controls the faucet on the shower. The gate keeper can stay over in my room while my mom is working."

"Josh, what's our mom going to say when you disappear for three days?"

"I'm sure you'll let us know Mikey." Ben laughed.

"What are you going to say to her Mikey?"

"That you two faggots ran away with each other."

CHAPTER TWENTY

A Man at Fourteen

When Benjamin returned to his house to pick up the book, he hoped that Josh had made it safely to the bookstore, after he left Mikey in the cyberspace room.

"Why do you call this the cyberspace room?" Josh asked Mikey.

"All the books in here are listed for sale on the internet." This is the Bookman's computer room."

"Do you work the computer?"

"We sell books on line, take orders and E-Mail the customers. Not only do we sell books from here but we list the titles with all the information about them."

"Which means you do all of this for the bookstore?"

"Sure Josh. Then after we send the E-Mail, holding the book they ordered, the customers pay us by mail or with a credit card. When they pay, I pack the books for shipping. I take them to the post office and mail them to the customers."

"You know how to use a computer Mikey?"

"He taught me how. What I do here is not taught in class Josh."

"This means Mikey, you know about quantum computers?"

"Sure Josh, but we don't have one here because they don't exist!"

"You've been putting me on all this time Mikey. What if there is a quantum computer in the secret room?"

"When's the last time the tooth fairy left you a quarter?"

Books

Benjamin rode home on his bike through the park. He walked into the kitchen where his mother sat listening to the radio.

"We have to talk Benjamin."

"Yeah mom, we do."

"Why didn't you tell me about Father Edwards? Why Benjamin, and what he did to Josh?"

"Did you ever think mom that children can protect their moms like moms can protect their children?"

"What do we do about all of this Benjamin? You can't go back to that school. Josh may end up in the detention center again. You seem to think you are a man, not a boy anymore. You are asking me to trust you when you and Josh come here tonight. You are asking me to let Josh's brother stay here every night for the next three nights. Then Benjamin, you want me to let all of

this happen without me asking any questions?"

"No mom. Ask anything you want to."

"This is your Grandfather's doing isn't it?"

"Yes."

"He sent you all those books to read since you have been able to read.

You read all of them?"

"Yes"

"I wanted you to be smart and go to college. He sends you a telescope

when you are seven. He sends you all these books each year. Answer me one

question Benjamin. Where do you keep all these books?"

"Above my closet there is a secret place."

"How many books do you have there?"

"You don't even want to know mom."

"They came in the mail while I was working?"

"Yes mom."

"Why didn't you show them to me?"

"Remember when Grandfather sent me "Catcher in the Rye?""

"You were only eight years old. That book was banned in the school library. Benjamin I was only protecting you!"

"Protecting me from what mom, the boogie man?"

"I only wanted you to keep your childhood and your innocence as long as possible. The church and the school authorities knew best Benjamin."

"Like Father Edward and Ms. Agnes the school librarian?"

"Mother's don't want their sons to grow up Benjamin. We want to protect our children from the real world."

"Like protect me from my real father?"

"Benjamin."

"Protect me from the books Grandfather sent to me?"

"No."

"Protect me from knowing about the stars and planets?"

"I love you Benjamin."

"You are a real part of my life mom. You don't have to protect me from the real world."

"Now what are we going to do?"

"Good question mom. We have some things to do tonight. Josh and I will be in my room and Mikey will be upstairs with us. Trust us mom. That is all we ask."

"Why should I Benjamin? There has been nothing but trouble since the three of you got together."

"You have only one reason mom to trust us."

"What's that Benjamin?"

"I love you too mom."

CHAPTER TWENTYONE

Officer Sherwood

Chief of Police Fairchild met with Officer Sherwood at eleven o'clock on Saturday **morning. Sherwood was tense.**

"This shift program last night didn't seem to work out hey Sherwood?"

"No sir. Not exactly liked we planned."

"Seems that we have a report from last week on you jumping a pregnant female?"

"She resisted arrest sir."

"This was a routine traffic stop?"

"She jumped out of the car sir. I wasn't sure if she had a gun."

"So you knocked her down and, let me see here, you pounced upon her. Do we jump on a suspected felon officer Sherwood? Is that our standard procedure?"

"No sir. It isn't"

"Was there another officer with you at the time?"

"No sir."

"Did you call for back up?"

"She was alone sir. No need for backup."

"Looking at last night's shift report Sherwood, you were not to go on patrol, but were given specific tasks for investigating the activities of three boys in the village. Isn't that true?"

"Yes sir. I was."

"And did you accomplish these duties?"

"No. No sir."

"Please explain why not Officer Sherwood."

"First of all sir, these boys have been running around the streets. We bring them in here at least once a week to question them."

"Why?"

"It's what we do. They are streetwise sir. These kids are a source of information."

"You bring them into this station and question them without their parents present?"

"You have to understand chief. They are from bad homes. None of them have a father around and the mother is on welfare."

"I'll let this one go, for now Sherwood. The man who runs the Bookstore on the corner; No one seems to know who he is. According to the owner of the pawn shop across the street from the bookstore, boys are going in and out of that place."

"The pawn shop sir?"

"Your shift report requested you investigate the relationship of the boys, whose mother's you were to interview last night, and the boy's relationship to the man who is running the bookstore."

"The mothers were not available sir."

"Then who did you talk to?"

"One of the boys in the store, named Mikey. He is one of the boys' whose mother was on the list."

"He works there, in the store?"

"Yes sir. He told me the other two boys, his brother and the other boy on your list were at his house."

"What did you do next?"

"We went there and found that no one was home. When we went back to the bookstore it was closed. Officer Mitchell swore the boys bikes were on the sidewalk but just disappeared while I was in the store talking to the youngest boy."

"Then you both decided to patrol Chemung Street?"

"No sir. We went to the home of one of the boys. Mitchell and I asked for backup. It was just to scare the little pricks sir. They really did a number on the church school today. They terrorized the faculty meeting."

'Was the mother home?"

"Yes sir. She wouldn't let us in and she said we needed a warrant if we wanted to get in her house."

"Have you ever been in her house?"

"Yes sir, we investigated once when the boy called in a false alarm. We couldn't prove it."

"Did you see any old interesting furniture?"

"It seemed like a lot of junk to me sir, all wooden oak stuff. Why?"

"Well my hobby is collecting and selling antiques."

"We would need a search warrant chief."

"Our elected magistrate would not give us a warrant to enter her place. She refused to speak to us."

"They will surface tomorrow. Issue an alert for those troublemakers. Father Edwards is a good friend of mine. What they did to him today is unforgivable. A warrant to search the house can wait until we bring the boys in for questioning with their mother's present."

"They won't talk chief. We tried."

Chief Fairchild smiled ending the interview with Sherwood.

"We have to find one of those three juveniles who will talk to us." The Chief said.

Sherwood turned as he left the office. "There is one mother who will help us chief. She has two sons."

"Set it up with her Sherwood. You can plant the evidence we need in that bookstore."

"Yes sir."

CHAPTER TWENTYTWO

Mom becomes a Rocket Scientist

Benjamin, Mikey and Josh waited to see if Mrs. Winslow let the officers in the house. They listened from upstairs until they heard the patrol cars drive away. Benjamin explained to his mom earlier that some policemen might stop by to talk to them.

"You aren't going to clue me in on any of this are you Benjamin? Just like your Grandfather, you won't let me know what it is that is going on here."

Benjamin's mother called them to come down once the policemen left.

"You may as well finish the cookies." She told them when they entered the kitchen.

Josh poured more milk into his glass. "Mrs. Winslow, you don't want to know. If we let you know, Mikey would be compromised."

"Compromised? What is that supposed to mean?"

"Mom, listen to what Josh is telling you. Benjamin put his hand on her shoulder. "In three days we will sit down here, at this table, and explain what is going on."

"Why can't I know now?"

Officer Sherwood is going to search this house tomorrow along with his buddies. When they are finished you have to go to work like nothing happened. Mikey will stay in my room after school. In three days we will be back here. Just send Mikey to school in the morning. He knows what to say and what to do."

"What if they take him away?"

"Just go to the Bookman and he will get him back mom."

"Why?

"Mikey is going to make sure you are safe. He is our gate keeper."

"So he is in on this too. Your grandfather is behind this. The man you refer to as 'The Mountain Man', is he in on this also?"

"He is so great mom. You are just going to love him!"

"But where is he. Can I see this invisible man?"

"The Mountain Man is like what most of the Universe is." Benjamin told his mother.

"Which is?"

"Invisible."

"Like the truth." Mikey said.

"Right," Benjamin told her, "Just like we will be tomorrow for three days."

"The truth is invisible?" She asked them.

"Like the truth you kept from me about dad for many years mom. Like all the truth all around us that everyone seems to keep from us every day."

"We have to protect you Benjamin. Many times the truth can hurt you."

"Sure." Mikey said. "Government calls it national security. Policemen call it the right to know. Priests call it Faith in the teachings of the church."

"Know the truth and it shall make you free!" Josh cried.

"Where did you boys learn all this foolish nonsense?" She asked.

"From books mom, those damn books. They can make you crazy."

The boys stood up and danced around the table. "Burn his books Father. The man tilts at windmills. Burn! Burn his books!"

The boys cleaned up the kitchen mess and went to Benjamin's room.

In Benjamin's room they wrestled on the floor.

"Your mom thinks we are wacko." Mickey exclaimed.

"She knows that we are up to something." Jason smiled.

"Well aren't we all teenagers now? Benjamin declared.

"Except for me guys," Mikey told them.

"We haven't forgotten that today you are thirteen!" Josh laughed.

They grabbed Mikey and pulled his pants down. Thirteen hard slaps later Mikey became a teenager.

They all headed into the bathroom. Mikey turned the shower handle to the left. "When you hear us knock on the wall, then close it." Benjamin told him. They listened to the sliding on the other side of the bathroom wall. Josh and Benjamin left Mikey, as they went into the bedroom.

Josh grabbed Benjamin's arm when Benjamin walked through the opening and started up the stairs.

"Wait." Benjamin said as he stepped back into his room. "Get the book on my bed. Mikey has to have a code for opening the door again. Benjamin went into the bathroom.

Mikey was sitting in the bathtub getting ready to light a cigarette.

"Don't worry Ben. When they leave and your mom is asleep you can come down from the room. Just knock on the wall man."

"Three knocks, then two, then one. OK?"

Josh and Benjamin walked slowly up the stairwell to the secret room. They knocked on the wall and stopped. The wall closed, surrounding them in darkness.

They heard a click as the wall stopped moving. Bathed in a green soft light they continued upward.

The articles in the room glowed as they boys entered the illuminated dome. Computers surrounded them giving off colors they had never before seen.

"Whatever this is," Josh whispered, "isn't the stuff you find in the world below us."

"Look at the dome above us." Benjamin said. "All of the glittering stars in the universe!"

"Wow!" Josh cried. "They are like waves, an ocean of stars."

"They disappear like waves reaching a shore, over and over again."

"This is so weird Benjamin. It is like the best feeling ever."

"They are singing to us Josh. Can you feel it?"

"They make me feel no end to myself Benjamin. This is so beautiful!"

"Like there is no end to any of this."

"Or even us."

"What are those beautiful lights Josh?"

"Grandfather told me I would discover the mysterious scroll of the universe."

"He is right Ben. The calculus tells me it is so. Pythagoras told his students that mathematics was how we were able to understand the real world." His mathematics created music. Music defied the teachings of the priests."

"Pythagoras created another language."

"Grandfather told me there was another language most men did not understand."

"It was a mathematical language where sounds were created to express our feelings.

"Like the mating calls of animals?" Ben asked.

"Yes. Like the crickets, the song birds and the bull frogs. As we listen I can understand the mysteries of our own instruments."

"Josh you cannot mean what it is you are telling me?"

"Yes. Most of us in our ignorance, cannot grasp so much, or see so far, in order to penetrate the mysteries of our universe."

"Mikey will not agree."

"Our gate keeper needs to see this Ben."

"You need to show it to him Josh."

"Ben. You don't smoke. Why don't I open the wall while Mikey joins us as you look this place over?"

"Why don't we all see it together?" Ben asked.

"Remember that click Ben when the door closed?"

"Yeah, that's when all these lights came on Josh."

"That is why the Bookman said we need a gate keeper. If someone walks up these stairs without the gatekeeper turning the handle to the left, this cannot be seen."

"This is the Secret Room Ben!"

"When Mikey sees this he will guard it well."

CHAPTER TWENTYTHREE

Monday Morning

Officer Sherwood sat in an unmarked car across the street from Benjamin's house. He was off duty. Knowing one of the boys had to leave for classes he parked facing the school.

None of them were seen over the weekend. Checks on both of their houses and the bookstore found no sign of anyone.

The school filed trespassing charges against Josh even though Josh was placed on detention, in the office, at the time the door was locked. Charges were filed against Mikey for the damage to the globe in the library.

At the police station Father Edward met with the Chief to form a plan of action against Benjamin. They sat in the chief's office waiting for the magistrate to arrive.

"The boy had no right to record our conversation." Father Edward told them. "He was sent by his mother."

"He didn't ask your permission?"

"He came to my office and walked in without knocking first!"

"There isn't anything illegal about recording a conversation with you Father."

"He had no right to play the tape over the school's PA system."

"His friend Josh played it Father. Benjamin could be put on the carpet for playing the tape but it wasn't he who did it."

Magistrate Wolfe walked into the office. "Morning Chief. What's so important you got me down here at this hour?"

"Morning Judge. You know Father Edward here. There is some problem at school which needs looking into." The Chief said.

Explaining the events of the previous Friday, Chief Fairchild let Father Edward continue.

"This boy is accusing me of wrongdoing Judge. Listen to this recording!"

Chief Fairchild played the tape. The judge sat in silence thinking.

"This seems to be a very disturbed child Father."

"How can we stop these false accusations your honor?"

"Have you talked to the mother?"

"Yes. She is as crazy as her son. He gets his ideas from her, a woman living alone without a man, raising a troubled teenager."

"We ought to get the Assistant DA in on this Wolfe." Chief Fairchild suggested.

"No. No Chief. He has enough on his hands. He owes me a few favors anyway. This attempt to destroy Father Edward and the Holy Church must not go beyond this room."

"This can't get around the church your honor. My ministry will..."

"Father Edwards. Not to worry. Here is what we will do." Wolfe told the priest.

"Get the boys here with their mothers. Two of the boys have been before me on prior disciplinary charges. This third boy, Benjamin Winslow, does he have a record of delinquency?"

"He's clean." The Chief told them.

"We do this all the time Chief." The Judge told him. "Scare the mother. Tell her we will take her son away if he doesn't shut his mouth."

"You can do this?" Father Edward asked them.

"To bring all this nonsense to an end Father, yes we can. Somewhere down the line you have to be a witness. We are the law here, not the Constitution.

"Witness to what?"

"Whatever it is we can bring up against the boy and his mother."

"Your honor, what if she hires a lawyer?"

"Not on her salary Father. We always win these cases with the poor

mother's. They just give up their rights and move to another town."

What about the Public Defender?"

In this village the Public Defender is usually, in addition to his law practice,

a local business man such as an Optometrist or a professional with a law degree

unable to support his Shingle hanging outside his office.

Father Edward smiled. "Protect and serve your honor?"

"Our Public Defender earns most of his fees when his cases are lost."

"The worst boys eventually turn sixteen. Then we can sentence them to

serve inside the county jail until they see it our way."

"I cannot wait until these boys are sixteen." Father Edwards told him.

"Didn't we protect your ass Father when the one boy tried to chew your

dick off?"

"Somehow this boy Benjamin, who recorded the false tape, is different. The mother is different from the rest of them. She is a real fighter your honor. It's like she is using her son to destroy me."

"That, father, is why we have the Officer Sherwood's of this world. He finds a way to break them down, find their weaknesses and deliver them to my court."

"With charges pending, they almost always see it our way." The Chief laughed.

A dispatcher entered the office and handed the Chief a note. "Well father Edward, Officer Sherwood tells us your first boy is riding his bike to school. Isn't it time for you to go over there and talk to him?"

The judge stood up. "Have the boy and his mother here after school. We wouldn't want him not to learn his lessons."

They laughed as the dispatcher returned to the radio room.

CHAPTER TWENTYFOUR

Benjamin and Josh

"Edgar Allen Poe wrote <u>The Maelstrom,</u> a tale of this man being sucked into a whirlpool as he sat in his boat off the coast in the Atlantic Ocean. He waited for his fate as his row boat circled, swirling him deeper into the vortex of the water."

"Is this another one of the books Grandfather sent you?" Josh asked.

"No Josh. Read me the paragraph on black holes, the one Bookman checked in Fuller's first volume."

"*According to Hawking, the assertion that nothing, even light, can escape from a black hole is not strictly true. Weak thermal energy does radiate from around black holes…Before the matter-antimatter particles can recombine and annihilate each other, one that may be slightly closer to the black hole will be sucked in, while the other that is slightly farther away escapes as heat…*"

"Stop," Benjamin interrupted. Poe's character escapes death from being sucked into the vortex. He notices that certain objects swirling around the vortex are floating upward. He grabs onto one of them, a barrel of rum, and ties himself to it. He lives. According to the story, he has aged many years. His hair turns white even though he is only twenty some years old."

"This has something to do with quantum physics Benjamin, a story written by some drunk in the 19th century?"

"It is the law of quantum physics Grandfather mentioned. Everything that happens in the universe is interconnected to everything else."

"Like Father Edwards? What we did to him? What he did to me? What he is going to do to our butts next time he sees us?"

"He can't touch us now. Our priest is history."

"What about Mikey, he is probably in school while we are safe in here? Josh asked.

"This room will give us the answer." I'm sure of it Josh."

"There is something here I never saw before Ben."

"There is a future for us Josh, which includes Mikey."

"The future is ours. That's all we can ask for Ben."

"Our gatekeeper is going to open the door when he returns from school today."

"What if he doesn't return Ben? Are we trapped here forever?"

"Not if we can understand how to work these computers Josh."

"Like we are such hackers Ben, not even Bill Gates knows about these machines."

"Don't be too sure about that"

"What do we do next?" Josh asked.

"Grandfather didn't set this up for us to be losers here Josh."

"We've always been losers Benjamin; Mikey, you and me and two mothers who don't have a decent man at home helping us."

"My grandfather is a decent man Josh."

"Yeah but he isn't there every night keeping you from being a couch potato."

"You have a point there. Mom would never let him live with us. She doesn't want me to go through what she went through while she was growing up." Benjamin told him. "She always thought he was a nut."

"Well that makes three of us Ben. What are we doing here? How do we make it out of here? What is going on? Maybe we need to be taking care of our moms."

"Our moms will be just fine when we get through this."

"If we get through this," Josh said, what is the next step?"

"These are the problems grandfather gave us Josh. Do you have any answers?"

"No Ben but we have some new theories here."

"Yeah well I kind of like this room. Do you get the feeling someone is watching us?"

If you want to solve the problems Ben then we need to explain them."

"You want some of my theories on this Josh?"

"Sure."

"What happens when a theory is proven?" Ben asked him."

"It becomes a law."

"That's what is out there on the other side of this wall, the law!"

"What law?"

"It is Father Edward's law, Officer Sherwood's law, Ms. Agnes's law and the law of the bullies running the world." Ben explained.

"What about our own law? All of us have the right to be whatever we choose to be?" Josh told him.

Benjamin looked into the sky dome of the room. "Not in our dimension Josh, not when we must be what everyone says we must be."

"We can be anyone we want to be. We just have to be willing to deal with the consequences."

"What if the consequences are harmful?"

"Millions of men have died choosing to suffer the consequences." Josh said.

"There is someone definitely watching us and listening to what we say. I can feel it." Ben said.

"Do you want to hear my theory Ben?"

"Will it become a law?"

"Probably not, but here it is anyway. Every time I wanted to be someone or do something right for me, it turned out against me. They locked me in my room, put me in detention, and even put me in a juvenile jail. My theory is this. If life is smacking you in the face find some books to escape with. Find your own mountain man. Most important Ben, never, never, never quit trying to be what it is you want to be, and you will become whatever it is you want to be!"

"Damn Josh. There is a law for your theory. Grandfather calls it a tenet of clear thinking.

"What is it Ben?"

*"Do whatsoever you will, shall be the full extent of the law."**

"Daring men and women throughout the centuries Ben dared to challenge the law?"

"What about our Moms?"

"It must be very painful for mothers to follow the law Ben."

"Especially when they agree that the law has the right to send their sons off to fight the wars."

"We never talked like this before. It must be this room." Josh said.

"What about your law when you tried so hard not to be like others Jason?"

"It was only a theory. You came up with the law."

"The law works in the third dimension Josh. What do you suppose happens when you apply fourth dimensional laws to your theory?"

"My theory is third dimensional, so any theory proven is a third dimensional law."

"Where did this wonderful theory of yours lead us to Josh?"

"We cannot break the laws Benjamin without suffering the consequences.

Even your Grandfather told you this!"

Another voice in the room spoke to them. "Welcome to the fourth

dimension fellow travelers."

CHAPTER TWENTYFIVE

Mikey is Taken Prisoner

Mikey entered his homeroom class. As he walked to his desk the other students cheered. His teacher, Mrs. Wilkinson, raised her hand and glowered.

"Mikey. You are to report to the office now."

"What if I don't want to go?" He asked her.

The class laughed, but was silenced as Mrs. Wilkinson slapped her desk with the blackboard pointer. She took a deep breath and spoke.

"In thirty years of teaching no student ever asked that question. You have to go Mikey."

"Why?" He asked.

"You will go because I say so!" Officer Sherwood stood in the doorway of the classroom. "Bring your book bag with you and follow me."

The students looked at the officer then turned their eyes from the policeman to Mikey.

"You ain't in charge here." Mikey told him.

"Mikey please go with him. Please." The teacher pleaded.

Why?" He asked.

"Yes why?" One of the students asked her.

"Because he asked you to, she replied. "He has authority to take you, don't you officer?"

Sherwood entered the room and went over to Mikey's desk.

Mikey put his hands on the desk. "Take me cop. Ever hear of passive resistance?"

"No! No! Please Mikey just go with him." His teacher cried.

Suddenly, the other students left their desks and surrounded Mikey, blocking Officer Sherwood.

Mrs. Wilkinson went to the wall phone and called the office.

The policeman walked through the circle of students. Reaching under Mikey's arms, he lifted him onto his shoulders. Officer Sherwood was not prepared for what happened next.

The Principal's Office

Chief Fairchild raised his hand and brushed back the hair on his head between his fingers.

"I just don't understand this sir."

" You are the principal here and this is your jurisdiction.

Why do you think my officer is responsible for all of this?" The chief asked.

"Officer Sherwood had no right to enter the classroom without my permission! Why was he here in the first place?"

"He was doing his job sir."

"Which is, may I ask Chief?"

"Serve and protect."

"This is too much! Too much"

"What is too much of what?" The chief asked.

"Excessive force, police force, you know very well what I am talking about."

"We have a serious situation here Mr. Principal."

"What is next chief? Are you going to bring in the county swat team?"

"No sir, at least not yet, please calm down. We still haven't found Officer's Sherwood's gun."

"Nor his night-stick and if I may add his pants are gone also!" Principal Crispen added.

"It is a matter of time. We will question each one of these kids and get to the truth." The chief told him.

"Chief, many of these children are cared for with only one parent at home. Half of them are on Ritalin. They run the streets after school looking for cigarettes or whatever it is they can't get at home."

"It was in this school they attacked my officer, tore his pants off and took away his belt with the equipment attached. In case you forget the officers carry mace, guns, cuffs, radios, night sticks and arrest pads, all of which were taken today from Officer Sherwood.

Officer Sherwood had no right to be in this school today unless he checked into the office first, which he did not! The administration, the church, cannot be responsible for what happened to him."

"Tell me," Chief Fairchild asked, "If one of your students came in here with a gun would we need your permission to go the classroom where this criminal was holding a class hostage?"

"That is oranges and apples chief. Mikey is not a criminal. He didn't have a gun. This boy was not holding the class as hostage. The class was protecting him. Your officer had the gun, not the student."

The chief looked toward the outer office where Mikey was being handcuffed by two policemen.

CHAPTER TWENTYSIX

Star Charts – The Room - Calculus

"Benjamin."

"Yes Josh."

"Are you sure this man is your Grandfather?"

"Yes."

"We have to make some sense out of all of this. You understand?"

"Sure. We will Josh one step at a time."

"First Benjamin we have this endless sky above us with, like, zillions of

stars. They can't be real. So this must be a planetarium."

Benjamin put his hands together and looked up.

"Are you praying?" Josh asked.

"No. I'm just thinking. Here is how this plays. There are the heavens

above us. What we see, we are, the stars and planets and suns. We are the

seeing them at the same time in the same place. Everything above us, our

seeing it all and what we are is the same." Benjamin tried to explain.

"We are in a different dimension with those lights Ben. They shine on us.

We see them as they are but with different minds." Josh was suddenly silent.

"We are no longer in the third dimension."

"Yes Josh. We are still in the third dimension but now both of us are at the same time living in another dimension. We have reached the fourth dimension."

"What is the first step? I wonder if Mikey could see us now, would he understand?"

"We have discovered a new language in the calculus. Next we figure out how to chart the maps. Grandfather said we would be able to follow the directions on this new computer."

"The next step Benjamin is getting back to our gatekeeper. Mikey needs a cell phone so we can talk to him."

"How are we going to get cell phones?"

They looked at each other. Together they said, "The Bookman!"

"It is time to show Mikey this room. What time is it Ben in the third dimension?"

Benjamin looked in his Map Book. He scanned the dome above the room. "It is noon, Saturday."

Benjamin knocked on the wall to the bathroom. They watched the wall open then stepped into the bedroom. Mikey ran into the room and stood in front of the opening.

"You two can come down now." He said.

"We are down Mikey!"

Mikey looked around the room. "You guys aren't pulling tricks on me, are you?"

"We are going to the bookstore and get some cell phones so we can talk to you no matter where you are." Josh said.

"That sounds good to me Josh except I can't see you or Benjamin. Do I stay here or what?"

"You stay in the house until you go to school Monday morning. The gatekeeper stays by the gate." Benjamin said. "Where is my mom?"

"She went out for some groceries and to get her hair done."

Mikey told them what happened in school.

"Who bailed you out?" Josh asked.

"Your mom Ben, she went to the Bookman.

They let me out when your mother said she would call the county judge about Officer Sherwood walking into the classroom with his gun."

"Officer Sherwood isn't too smart." Ben laughed.

"He smacked me on the back of the head when the magistrate set me free."

"Can we get you anything?" Josh asked.

"You know what I like Josh. If they don't have menthols then regulars will do."

"Nobody will sell them to us Mikey!"

"They won't have to." Mikey said.

"There is something wrong with him." Josh told Benjamin. "When he speaks to me he looks right through me."

"What's wrong Mikey?" Benjamin asked.

"Wrong! You are asking me if something's is wrong?"

"Yeah Mikey, that was what the question was." Josh asked.

"I can hear both of you but I can't see you." Mikey told them.

"Step three?" Josh said.

The Bookstore

When they entered the bookstore the small brass bell tinkled above them.

"Another angel just got its wings." Josh said.

"Very funny Josh," Ben said, "considering how you got the cigarettes."

"You call that funny Ben.

Funny is us standing across the street looking into the hair dresser's window while she is working on your mom."

"Not as funny as Officer Sherwood walking out of the pawn shop right in front of us talking to himself."

"He didn't notice the money he rolled up and put in his pocket as he crossed the street." Ben laughed.

"When he dropped the ten dollar bill on the sidewalk you snatched it up before he knew it was falling."

"The cigarettes were expensive. You could have at least taken change from the register for that ten you put in."

"The guy who works there will be over in his count tonight He will probably stick it in his pocket."

"Nice diversion there Josh while the smokes slid out of the case."

"Figured a few Playboys and Playgirls falling on the floor would get his attention."

"Did you see that Hustler Magazine?"

"Do fish swim Josh?"

"Do birds fly?"

Step IV

They did not see the Bookman when they entered the store. Walking to the cyberspace room, Josh stopped next to the globe sitting on the front counter. "Hey Ben," he called, "This globe shows Viet Nam on the map instead of French Indo China."

"Can you pick it up Josh?" Ben asked as he disappeared into the back room.

Josh lifted the globe. It was not as large as Ms. Agnes's. He thought of buying it for the librarian. He put it down thinking there would never be enough money in his pocket to replace her ancient outdated globe she kept in the school library.

"It was a good idea while it lasted." Josh thought to himself. He worked his way along the stacks until he came to the computer room.

Benjamin sat next to the Bookman who was entering data into the computer. Books were piled around him in stacks sitting on the floor. "Almost done he told the two boys."

"He sees us." Ben said.

"Why am I not surprised?" Josh sighed.

"You seem to be handling this infinitesimal matter really well Benjamin said."

"The Bookman smiled. "Are you geniuses ready to handle infinity?"

"Only if infinity is infinitesimal and you have cell phones" Josh told him.

"You mean two railroad tracks which never touch?" The Bookman asked.

"What about two parallel lines going into infinity without meeting?" Benjamin asked.

"Oh how sad." The Bookman laughed.

"Why sad?" Josh asked him.

"The wonderful things with railroad tracks are the switches. They allow endless meetings in order to get where they are going."

"You sure know my Grandfather." Benjamin told the Bookman.

"This is not a philosophy session." The Bookman told them." "Josh. Here is a question for you concerning the new dimensional calculus."

"What?" Josh asked."

"What do you know so far about the language of dimensional calculus?"

"That it is beyond words. The mind has to think in other terms, terms other than signs and symbols we learned in the third dimension unlike the one we are in now."

"You are still in the third dimension Josh. The difference is that you have also entered the next dimension. Mathematically, the fourth dimension calculus formulas are very different."

"We can talk to Mikey but he can't see us. How is it our sound is here but not our light?"

"Josh! Think about the answer to that one."

"Sound is at the far end of the light spectrum?"

"Sound is on the same wavelength as light but very low on the scale. You cannot be seen above the speed of light." The Bookman told them.

"We cannot see sound," Benjamin said, "unless we use a light spectrum."

"Nor can we hear light waves." Josh added. We never see any object or person. It is only the light reflecting from everyone and everything that is visible. Not all of the light spectrum can be seen by the human eye nor can we hear all of the wave lengths of sound." He told them.

"The speed of light is much faster in the fourth dimension?" Josh asked.

"In the fourth dimension the speed of light is twice the speed of light in the third dimension. That is why Mikey could not see you."

The quantum calculus here is the important thing. You both need to know how important this project of ours is and what it is."

"Why involve us in this project?" Josh asked.

"We need those who will learn the calculus and astronomical maps in order to take this world to the next one. For many years we have worked on the means to achieve our goal of saving this planet, or what is left on this planet, preventing total destruction."

"You mean the destruction of earth?" Benjamin asked.

"Your Grandfather will explain the details. For now it is my task to assist you in reaching the launching pad of this project."

"How will men destroy the earth?" Josh asked the Bookman.

"By landing upon and destroying Earth's Moon."

"This is the reason for the Secret Room?" Josh asked.

"It is only one of the staging areas of our project. Many young men and women are now being trained to build a ship which will travel to the next galaxy."

"Why did you pick Benjamin and me?"

"That will be explained later."

"Are we going through some kind of test to see if we can do these things you ask?"

"The tests have come and gone. Each one of you passed every test. Most of them you never knew about."

"We were guinea pigs?" Josh asked.

"No Josh. When you passed each test you gave us permission to go on."

"How could you know?"

"By you picking up those books and reading them. If you never wanted to know about the next dimension you would have discarded the books we placed in front of you, and gone back to the street."

Josh walked out of the room. He came back and opened his eyes as wide as he could.

"When the judge and Father Edward stuck me in that detention center you knew about me?"

"They thought that by allowing you to play games on the computers you would become less aggressive. Instead you went on line and found us."

"They never knew what was available to me on the internet. One night, feeling very sad, I sang 'Where Oh Where is Love.' It was from the Movie, 'Oliver', which they showed us in the school gym.

In the juvenile jail I was turning the computer off for the night when one of the screws called me to bed. The monitor beeped and a light flashed. The words read, "**Josh. Not in your pocket but in your mind. Go to Sunflower.com tomorrow night at this time.**"

"Then what happened?"

"For the first time since they stuck me in that place, my hope grew to even think there was someone out there caring for me, weird as it was."

"You never told me this Josh." Benjamin said.

"You never told me you were keeping a star map book Ben."

"So what happened next?"

"The following night the guard left me alone in the computer library. Logging on to Sunflower.com changed my whole life."

"What happened?"

"Whoever they were, they sent me books, books on all kinds of subjects. Stories told about adventures, novels written for children my age, lots and lots of books."

"You read all of them?"

"Yes. Then one day the sergeant in charge of the library told me the books had to stop coming. My assigned locker was full. There was no room in the library he told me, when I asked him to take the books there. They were removing the books to make way for additional computers.

What could I say? The computer was the reason I found Sunflower.Com. What did they do?"

"They sent the books back to wherever they came from."

"They came from here Josh. Mikey mailed most of them to you. When the county mailed them back to us, The United States Postal System delivered them here with postage return due. They wanted me to pay for books, which they were paid to deliver, and pay once more in order to get them back."

"So did you pay them?"

"No. I figured someone would take them home and read them. Books are written and published to be read."

Josh was amazed. "When they released me from the center and sent me home, Mikey brought me books. He started working here right before they let me go. At first he brought me fiction. Then he gave me books on math. It wasn't long before the books were about higher math. Math always made sense to me. Calculus kept me in some kind of trance. Mom never minded that I was locked in my room at night. She had other problems so it wasn't so bad for her to have me off the streets after dark. It worked out."

Step V

The Bookman gave us the cell phones with instructions. Because we were still new at this, we did not question how we could carry third dimensional objects such as cell phones and cigarettes while we were invisible.

It was established that Josh and I would work in the room until Monday evening. We were to learn how the new quantum computer worked. The only thing we knew about this computer was the spin-based chip developed by IBM. It was able to store data without drawing power. In other words, no batteries were necessary and it did not depend on the power from the circuit breakers in

the house. Neither Josh nor I realized the importance of this until much later,

when the Federal Agents turned the power off to the house.

We left the bookstore.

Josh and I walked into the kitchen as I closed the door. We found it was

not necessary to open or close doors but he said it was important not to sneak

up on his brother.

Mikey sat next to Benjamin's mom eating some chicken and potatoes.

Another surprise for us! We were not hungry. The Bookman told us that we had

to return to the third dimension in order to nurture our bodies. We stood there

as Mikey stuffed another spoonful of mashed potatoes into his mouth.

"Where do you suppose they are?" My mother asked.

"They are very safe Mrs. Winslow. Remember they are meeting us here

on Monday night."

"Will they be here for dinner? Where will they eat?"

"Wish my mom cared about us like you do."

"Your mother met me on the street today in front of the grocery store."

"She bought groceries?"

"No. She asked if you and Josh were staying here."

"Josh always does the shopping."

"Josh?"

"He gets the food stamps which come in the mail before Eric does. If he doesn't spend them when they come in the mail he tries to sell whatever is left at the end of the month in order to pay for booze and cigarettes."

"You mean you run out of food? What do you do?"

"We just crash anywhere there is food on the table. It's no big deal. You learn to deal with it." Mikey told my mom.

"How did you do that?"

Mikey was not going to rat on Benjamin. He fed both Mikey and his brother many times while she was at work.

Josh walked over next to his brother and whispered in his ear. "We got them."

Mikey pretended to scratch his ear and finished eating. "Can I go upstairs now Mrs. Winslow?"

"Sure. Just let me know when they get back. A promise is a promise, and I promised Benjamin you could stay here until Monday night."

"Thank you." Mikey said. He put his plate in the sink and went upstairs to Benjamin's room.

Step VI

"This isn't going to work out!" Mikey told them. "Your mother is just too nice."

"Of course she is nice. Why do you think you are here?"

"Nice mothers don't win ball games Ben."

"Nice mothers don't play ball games."

They gave Mikey the phone and told him how to use it. "What about my cigarettes? You think I'm going to be cooped up here in a bathtub without smokes?"

"There are no sacrifices here for you huh Mikey?" Josh asked his brother.

"I could be over at Greg's playing games on the computer."

"What computer?" Josh asked. Open the door Ben and we will show him a computer."

"Which one of us will take him up there?" Benjamin asked."

"You do it Ben. These aren't my brand of cigarettes, but beggars can't be choosy."

Josh walked out of the room. The wall slid open.

"Are you ready for this Mikey?" Benjamin asked.

"Do I have to do this?"

"What good is a gatekeeper if the gatekeeper doesn't know what the gatekeeper is keeping?"

CHAPTER TWENTYSEVEN

Grandfather

"We work so hard to place these aggressive boys in a safe environment."

"Sunflower.com could have been a scam to get the boys off track."

"Our Web Site has not been invaded yet."

"You saved your own grandson from them. They were going to destroy him."

"That was a close one. Chicago was a good place for the government considering the ethnic population.

Ethnic euthanasia was a government program to eliminate your grandson.

"Killed you mean?"

"What authority were they using then?"

"They used the Chicago Public School District to interview six year old boys."

"What was the name of the organization saving your grandson?"

"They were the Sisters of Mercy. They faked the execution of my grandson."

"He is the one at our Star Gate?"

"He will map the way for the 'Sunflower' once we launch the way to the next galaxy."

"We have not been successful with many of the dimensional travelers."

"Is it because of the gatekeepers?"

"Yes Grandfather."

"The Government has unlimited funds."

"We have the ability to produce unlimited funds. You know the gold in the government vaults is ours for the taking. When the Sunflower enters the sun we do not want any of their stolen gold."

"The World Governments may have unlimited funds to prevent us from succeeding. However the sources of their monies are quickly diminishing as the earth suffers.

NASA exploding their bomb on the moon disturbed the tides and platelets which Luna controls on our Earth. Six major earthquakes, the Icelandic volcanic ash disaster and the shift of the plates in the Gulf of Mexico oil spill resulted from NASA's attempt to discover water on the moon.

"We have established the farm in Oregon where our project will be launched. For now, the travelers must succeed in training those who will build the **"Spaceship Sunflower."**

Bookman

"These books in our store are beginning to frighten the authorities Grandfather. Why did you ever choose this village to set up the room?"

"It is in this village that our Gatekeeper lives. My daughter lives here with the grandson we saved many years ago. How lucky we are to find a boy like Josh who is able to learn Dimensional Calculus in such a poverty stricken town."

"The police are terrorists here Grandfather."

"The police are terrorists everywhere." Bookman told them."

CHAPTER TWENTYEIGHT

Particle Physics

Gravity works on all matter in the universe, at least the universe we know.

Giant galaxies are seen through very powerful telescopes. Astronomers chart

apter onetheir movements. The smallest particles discovered are seen in

powerful microscopes. Particle physicists have theorized the existence of

particles too small to be seen by any known instrument developed thus far. They

have yet to see ultrahigh-energy particles such as neutrinos or gamma-ray

photons and other sub atomic cosmic rays. Their work centers on a new

dimension.

Funding for telescopes versus micron spectrometers has always favored

the astronomers. The launching of probes into the sky touched the romantic

side of humankind. Outer space was the new frontier. The particle scientist

continued the search for the quantum computer finding it necessary, in order to

create the paths leading to other dimensions.

Many government agencies, especially the National Aeronautical and

Space Administration in the United States of America, funded the major probes

into space. The administrators in NASA were unaware of the contributions that the space labs contributed to the particle physicists, who changed robes and pretended to be astronomers.

Grandfather helped these scientists who otherwise would have returned to the streets where he found them. He gave them the title of Astrophysicists when they completed their degrees in one of the leading Universities in Chicago.

In the City of Chicago, Grandfather found a dumping ground of wasted minds turned out onto the streets by their school system.

It began in a Jazz café on Rush Street. One Saturday night Grandfather walked from one of his favorite restaurants to the cellar where a new ensemble gathered. On the sidewalk just outside the café two Chicago Policemen were questioning a boy who sat on what looked like a shoeshine box.

"Do you have a permit to shine shoes on the street?" The larger officer asked.

"No sir." The boy replied.

"Where is your mother kid?"

"She is in the shelter just down there." He pointed toward State Street.

"You can't get in there after 11 PM. They have a curfew." It's 1 AM and you can't get in the shelter after 11." The officer said.

"Yes I can get in anytime. I can get in sir."

The officers picked up the shoeshine box and riffled through its contents.

"So you make money shining shoes on the street without a permit?"

"Yes sir."

"How much money you got boy?"

"Some."

"You are selling drugs here?"

"I don't sell anything." The boy said.

The officer picked the boy up and stood him against the wall of the club.

Searching his pockets, the policeman found the money and took it from

him. "You need a permit to work on the street kid. Anyone tell you that?"

Grandfather watched them as the boy lowered his head not answering.

The officers walked back to the patrol car.

"We don't want to see you here anymore kid. Go back to the Southside

but don't come here anymore. Got it?"

Grandfather left the scene and entered the Café. He found his friend

Michael who was the head of the Astrophysics department at the University of

Illinois. Their table was next to the wall by the stage. They spent the night

listening to the sounds of the universe.

CHAPTER TWENTYNINE

Monday

Mickey was arrested in the school office by Chief Fairchild and taken to the village hall. By the time Judge Wolfe arrived Officer Sherwood entered the courtroom with his pants on.

"Why is the Assistant District Attorney present in this courtroom at a preliminary hearing? No one has been charged have they? The judge asked.

"Father Edward called me your honor. Our parish priest is disturbed by events taking place in our school."

As the District Attorney was speaking Father Edward came into the courtroom.

"More than events, it is more like a war against me your honor. These boys are out to destroy me!"

"You are not the only one under attack." Officer Sherwood joined in.

Judge Wolfe brought his gavel down to silence them.

"Perhaps you could tell us what this all about." He asked Chief Fairchild.

He pointed to Mikey. "It is this boy your honor. He is a large part of the problem. We sent an officer to the school in order to bring him in here for questioning. His mother is sitting over there." Chief Fairchild pointed her out to

the judge.

"He refuses to tell us where the other students are who helped him

destroy the globe in the school library. Two of them played a tape over the

school's sound system accusing Father Edward of attempted sexual abuse."

Father Edward jumped from his seat yelling. "The tape is not legal

evidence! It was doctored. They made it up!"

The Assistant District Attorney looked at the chief of police.

"Has your department investigated Father Edward's claims?"

"No sir we have not done so."

The District Attorney faced the judge. "Then why is this student here your

honor?"

"Today he caused a riot in his classroom. When Officer Sherwood walked

into his classroom to arrest him the students surrounded him. As the Officer

was lifting this student, who refused to walk with him, the other students

surrounded the officer and stripped him of his belt and pants along with all of his

equipment which included his gun."

"What happened next?" The DA asked.

"The officer was able to call for back up on his shoulder radio. That's when I entered the scene in the school office." The chief said.

Father Edward stood up once again "He is accusing me of trying to have sex with them!"

"I thought it was his other two friends Father?" The Assistant District Attorney asked.

"They are all in this together!"

Attorney Gerald suggested that Mikey be turned over to his mother until his next court appearance.

"No counselor!" Judge Wolfe disagreed. He will disappear just like his pals. This boy resisted arrest and has a record of delinquency."

"Then turn him over to the county. Get a child protective case worker over here to place him in protective custody."

Mikey pleaded with his mother to stand up for him and protest.

She lowered her head. "Maybe it is best for you." She told him.

The Bookman entered the courtroom.

Between the Law and the Court

"What are you doing in my courtroom?" The judge asked.

"I'm the boy's attorney your honor."

"Please show me the Attorney's License." The judge asked him.

The Bookman did as he was instructed.

The judge handed the card to the court clerk. "Copy this Margie."

"Your client is about to be charged with a felony."

"What felony?"

"He will be charged with resisting arrest and the unlawful taking of a weapon from a police officer."

"Where is the weapon?" the Bookman asked.

"We won't know until all of the children in the classroom are interviewed tomorrow."

"You are saying, your honor, that this officer entered a classroom in the state of New York with a firearm?"

The Chief of Police quickly stood up. "Officer Sherwood wasn't sure he had his gun with him."

The judge slapped his hand on the bench. "Case dismissed. This court is adjourned."

Monday Night

Mikey sat in the tub waiting. Three knocks, two knocks, one knock.

The gate keeper opened the door. Benjamin, Josh and Mikey gathered in the bedroom.

"Mom will be here in about thirty minutes." Benjamin said.

"We have to go down stairs and make it seem like everything is natural." Josh told them.

Step VII

"She expects us to be there tonight Mikey."

"Great Ben, you guys are somewhere in the sky above working on that computer. Why don't we just get the hell out of here? Tell your mom what's going on!"

"My Grandfather said if the gatekeeper freaks out, we have to start out all over again."

"Why?"

"There are people in government who don't want us to reach the next dimension."

"Why do we want to go to the next dimension Ben?"

"Why do men climb Mt. Everest Mikey?"

"For the same reason I climb a tree Ben, because it's there?"

"Yes Mikey. We want to go to the next dimension because it is there. You could have walked to the office with Officer Sherwood. There was nothing in your backpack to give us up."

"I know that."

"Then why didn't you go with him when he asked you to leave the classroom?"

"Mrs. Wilkinson gave me a sign."

"She was the one who wanted you to give up and go with Sherwood."

"She winked at me Ben."

"What gave you the balls to sit there and let Sherwood take you from your desk?"

"It was this room Benjamin, The Secret Room."

"Josh and I thought you would freak out Mikey when you saw the room."

"Why Ben, why would you guys think that?"

"We just didn't know Mikey how you would react."

"You guys kept me around you even though I didn't believe that there was such a place as another dimension Ben."

"We did that to you Mikey?" Josh asked

"Seems like everyone I really cared about doesn't want me to stay around. Not my father or my mother. The only ones who care about me are you and Josh and the Bookman."

"Stick with us Mikey. Josh and I think that you are the best gatekeeper in the universe."

"This is so great Ben. I could explode right now."

"Explode?"

CHAPTER THIRTY

Gateway to the Universe

Officer Sherwood knew Mikey was in Benjamin's house. He followed him there. Sherwood was certain he would also find Benjamin and Josh when he searched the house.

The judge was not going to issue a search warrant for the Winslow's place until one of Officer Sherwood's informants signed an affidavit stating that she bought her drugs from Benjamin's mother.

When the judge asked Officer Sherwood the name of the informant, Sherwood shrugged his shoulders. "She is the mother of the other two boys your honor."

"The mother of Father Edward's tormentors is your informant?" Is she reliable?"

"She has never been wrong yet Judge Wolfe, especially her boyfriend."

"The man I placed on probation for selling marijuana?"

"Yes Judge. We never could get anyone to testify against him when he was arrested. I found it on him."

"So what is it you hope to find in the other boy's house?"

"My informant tells me sir that the boy's mother keeps the bags of marijuana stashed in her bread box. We will search the house for her son Benjamin and his friend Josh. They have to be there. She is hiding them."

"What are the charges against them if you do find them?"

"Father Edward will file the charges your honor."

"You mean based on the tape being played in the school office?"

"Yes sir."

"When will you do this search?" the judge asked.

"We figure on surprising them around six tonight your honor."

"Which means Officer Sherwood that I will be called during my dinner, to come back here the arraignment?"

"Judge, we can hold these boys in our basement cages until you are ready to show up at the village hall."

"The state does not allow us to use the detainment cages officer!"

"We can use them in the case of violent prisoners' sir."

"You think that two 14 year old boys are going to be considered violent?"

"We have ways to make them violent your honor and it will be on tape."

"Will it show how you make them violent?"

"No sir. The tape will not start until they are really angry with us."

"Will Lt. Frank be responsible for this?"

"No Judge. He is still being investigated for the death of the 16 year old boy who stole the bicycle."

"The very reason we are not to use the cage rooms Officer Sherwood."

"Lt. Frank had nothing to do with that boy hanging himself in the cage your honor."

"Let us hope so. Meanwhile you wish to hold these two boys in the cage until my dinner is digested?"

"Yes your honor. You can smoke your cigar and have a brandy when you get home."

"Just how do you know about my personal habits officer?"

"Please your honor, this is a small village."

The warrant was issued.

As Officer Sherwood left the magistrate's office, the judge spoke. "You say this is a small village?"

"Yes sir I do?"

"My informants told me about last night?"

"You mean about what happened to me?"

"You were chased from the bar onto the street and knocked down. They say that you hit on a woman who was standing at the bar ignoring you."

"The chief gave me the assignment your honor. The woman I approached was not the suspect we were looking for. It was a case of mistaken identity sir. Ask Officer Mitchell!"

"The Chief tells me that the owner of the bookstore saw the incident. He went into the police station to report an "Officer down," even called 911."

"Officer Mitchell took two people into custody sir. He was under a lot of pressure when that Bookstore man came into the station."

"According to the Chief the Bookman thought Mitchell would try to rescue you from the crowd."

"He didn't have to your honor. The bar patrons were just playing around. We drink together and play darts every night when our shifts are over."

"You were on duty."

"Yes sir. It won't happen again."

The Warrant

Monday night Officer Sherwood rang the doorbell to Benjamin's place. The gatekeeper was prepared. He threw his cigarette butt into the toilet and picked up the cell phone. "Your mom is in the kitchen," Mikey said, "and it isn't Santa Clause at the door."

Benjamin spoke first.

"We still can't leave this room except through the sliding door. Josh can stay here, but knowing Sherwood, my presence is needed in the kitchen."

"What can you do?" Mikey asked.

"Remember how he planted that bag of grass in your house and Eric got taken into court? You took Eric's side Mikey."

"Benjamin. You are so out of it. Mom's boyfriend never had a penny to buy grass. He didn't have a job then. Our mom kept him in dope."

Sherwood just wanted to crush him Benjamin, because he was sleeping with our mom."

Josh grabbed the cell phone. "Look guys. The wolf or Wolfe is at the door. Let him in Mikey."

Benjamin's mother did not stand up when Mikey let Officer Sherwood and Mitchell into the room. Benjamin sat on the counter next to the microwave oven.

"Don't bother to show me the warrant." Benjamin's mother said.

"Finally, someone has some sense around here." Sherwood exclaimed. "Mitch you go check upstairs."

"Mrs. Winslow. You are in serious trouble." Officer Sherwood told her.

"Explain what you mean by trouble?" She asked him.

"We have reason to believe that you are hiding fugitives from justice and you are dealing in drugs."

Officer Sherwood stood with his back to the breadbox. Carefully he pulled a packet from his right pocket. He jammed it into the box next to a loaf of whole wheat bread and a package of muffins.

Officer Mitchell entered the kitchen. "There is nobody up there." He said. "This kid followed me into every room."

"I'm just keeping you cops honest." Mikey said.

Officer Sherwood moved over and poked his elbow into Mikey's arm.

"That attorney who saved you today will be history tomorrow!"

"Can tomorrow be history?" Mikey asked.

Officer Mitchell walked over and stood next to the breadbox.

"Are you hungry officer?" Mikey asked? "There aren't any donuts in that box."

Officer Mitchell turned and asked Sherwood if he could look inside the breadbox.

Sherwood pulled the warrant from his pocket and pretended to read.

"Yeah, says here she keeps the dope in the breadbox."

Benjamin's mother opened the breadbox and pulled the loaves out, placing them on the table.

The packet Officer Sherwood placed into the box was not there.

Step VIII

Benjamin sat on his bed. Josh was gathering the books from the hidden space in the closet. Mikey walked into Benjamin's room.

"That was close Benjamin!" Mikey said.

Josh walked to the opening in the wall. "What do we do with this grass?" He asked them.

Mikey smiled. "Sherwood might need this when we finish with him."

"How can you move this stuff without them seeing it? How do we have cell phones and they can't see them? Josh asked.

Benjamin sighed. "We cannot solve these mysteries. Grandfather says we can only experience them."

CHAPTER THIRTYONE

The Quantum Computer

"Time is relative." Benjamin said.

"Change is an illusion." Jason said.

"Fuller is difficult to understand!"

"Einstein is impossible!"

Jason and Benjamin were seated in front of the computer.

"It recognizes our voices and it can talk to us." Benjamin said.

Jason sighed. "Do you understand what it is saying?"

"Not quite. Not yet. But it is beginning to make sense." Benjamin replied.

"The past, the present and the future are an illusion Ben?"

"That's what Einstein said Josh"

"You mean that's what this computer said Einstein said."

"What is an illusion Ben?"

"You think something is there but it isn't."

"How can something not be there when you can run into it?"

"It is the dimension Josh, the dimension that the mind can travel beyond."

"Travel beyond what Ben?"

"Beyond the body it is in." Benjamin replied.

"We have to learn the calculus of the next dimension, dimensional calculus!" Josh said.

"Like board games or games played on the field."

"Right, the mind can move faster than the body it's in." Josh remarked.

"Like computer games?" Benjamin added.

"Illusions created by the mind." Josh said.

"Some bodies can move faster than others. Some minds can move faster than others."

"Then Einstien's mind moved faster than anyone's mind. He was seeking a unified theory to explain everything! This is so cool." Josh cried.

"He was probably thinking at the speed of light Josh."

"He didn't go into abstract non-verbal calculus then."

"Oh he did Josh. No one could keep up with his math in the 1950's."

"Or the speed with which his mind traveled?"

"That's it exactly, exactly what Buckminster Fuller was saying!" Benjamin said.

"Listen to this Ben. Fuller wrote, that in his Theory of Relativity, Einstein forged a far-flung connection between the geometry of space and time and the behavior of objects in motion within space and time."

The computer next to them clicked, buzzed and hummed.

"You are certain that you want to go on with this?" Quantum Computer asked them.

"What could be more exciting than being in this room?" Benjamin asked surprised, that a computer was able to carry on a conversation with them.

What to do With the Stash

"When is your Grandfather going to be here?" Josh asked.

"I don't know, but Mikey will be here soon."

"When he gets here, we can figure out what to do with this stash of mellow yellow that Sherwood left in our bread box.

Benjamin thought. "Do you have any ideas Quantum?"

CHAPTER THIRTYTWO

The Night Rockets

"You guys are just crazy!" Mikey said.

"Why?"

"Computers don't talk to people."

Josh sat on the toilet. "Remember when you called the phone company?" He asked Mikey.

"Yeah, the time they were going to disconnect us?"

"When you finished your conversation did you ever talk to a human voice, a real live person?"

"No."

"Yet you punched in all that information and found out that our phone was disconnected because mom didn't pay the bill."

"Then I pushed zero."

"Did a human answer?"

"A computer told me to wait."

"Computers do talk to people Mikey. The programs they use keep us from reaching a real person."

"They answer most of our questions Mikey. We can make a reservation or buy a toy without ever talking to another live voice."

Mikey lit his cigarette and sprawled inside the bathtub. "So you guys are saying that the computer up in the room talks to you?"

"The Quantum Computer in our room not only talks to us it can argue with us."

"It can tell us what we are thinking before we speak Mikey." Benjamin said.

"I want to talk to it." Mikey told them.

Josh looked at Benjamin.

"Really guys, if this machine can argue, then it needs to meet me."

"You don't stand a chance Mikey!" Josh said.

Benjamin left the bathroom stepping into the hallway. He stood with his back to them, and turning, he said, "Josh, our computer upstairs has the ability to debate with Mikey and whip his butt!"

"No Ben. If I know my brother, Quantum will have a major breakdown, for certain."

Mikey is Suspended

The three boys sat around the table in the kitchen. Mrs. Fontana's cookies were almost gone. Mikey poured another glass of milk. "So don't you guys like her cookies?" He asked.

"We don't eat right now." Josh said.

"It seems that we are in a state of suspended animation, or something like it." Benjamin told him.

"You mean hibernation?"

"We aren't asleep Mikey." Josh said.

"Fine with me, these cookies are great!"

"Tell us Mikey. What happened today? You still allowed in class?"

"Father Edward says there is no way my butt will be allowed in that school again."

"He is really pissed off about us then?"

"Sure. He started teaching sex education today. Male boys were put in a room where he could explain the birds and the bees to us."

"That's our Father Edward. He is a real hands' on teacher." Josh said.

"They expelled me." Mikey said.

"Why, for what we did to him with Ben's tape?"

"It was more than that. At the beginning of the class he asked me where you both were."

"What did you say?" Benjamin asked.

"He leaned into my face. His eyes looked me up and down. Then he stroked my hair."

"If you do not tell me where they are this will be your last class here." He said to me.

"He really is angry at us."

"When the class started, Father wrote some words on the blackboard. 'This is a class in 'sex education,' he told us."

Josh laughed. "He taught us all about sex last year!"

"Yeah," Benjamin added, "We found out that masturbation was immoral. If we felt the need to 'touch ourselves on God's gift to us', we were to go to him for help."

"So what did he say this year Mikey?"

"He asked us if we had anything to say about jerking off. He called it the moral sin against being a male in a world of carnal temptation."

"When he told us that last year, we just kept our mouths shut Mikey."

Josh told his brother.

"So?"

"So what did you say?"

"Well. Standing up to say something, my first thought was to walk out of the classroom."

Benjamin laughed. "But you just couldn't walk out of the room without saying anything?"

"Father," I asked, "Why don't we all jerk off and the first one who comes doesn't have to take this class anymore."

CHAPTER THIRTYTHREE

The Pawnbroker

Officer Sherwood sat on the stool in front of the Pawnbroker's counter. The Pawn Shop was directly across the street from the Bookstore.

"Where do you get all of this jewelry?" Sherwood asked.

"Off the street mostly." The Pawnbroker replied.

"People just come in here and sell it to you?"

"They need cash. I give them cold hard cash for the goods."

"Is any of the stuff stolen?"

"I'm sure it is but it isn't on any of the police chief's lists."

"Then it isn't on any of our department's burglar reports?"

"Not according to your Chief. He comes in here almost every day to check the items I buy off the street."

"But you don't show the Chief everything you buy."

"The Chief sends me a copy of his lists the day before he comes in to inspect."

"Where do the people who come in here to sell to you get it from?"

"They steal it mostly from their relatives. They steal it and bring it to me knowing that no questions will be asked."

"From what I hear you don't give them a lot for it." Sherwood said.

"My motto is, 'It ain't worth nothin' till I own it.'"

Officer Sherwood laughed. "Since you came to the village things haven't been the same."

"Especially not for you, now that we work together Sherwood." The Pawnbroker said.

Sherwood turned on his stool and looked out of the Pawn Shop window. "You are keeping a good eye on our man across the street?"

"What is he doing now?" The Pawn Broker asked.

"That's what we'd like to know."

"People go in to sell books. People go out with books. Some of them take books in. They must come out with cash just like my customers do."

"We know there is something going on in that bookstore besides books."

"This village is so dead. This is why I do well here because of the poverty and the lack of community spirit."

"Especially the drugs they buy from the cash you give them." Sherwood told him.

"Their need for drugs is the reason they come to me to exchange the gold and jewels for cash."

"We pay cash for information." Sherwood told the Pawn man.

"What kind of information?"

"We shake down the boys who run the streets, who know what their friends and parents are doing."

"Why doesn't the community, including your police department, give the boys a place to go after school?"

"What would they do?" Sherwood asked.

"Give them classes in arts, crafts, computers, that kind of stuff."

"Pawn Man. You are so funny. If we made those boys honest you would be out of business."

"Officer you are my kind of man. Now where is the bag?"

"We had a problem last night."

"What kind of a problem?"

"I put the bag in the mother's bread box like you suggested."

"Then you were able to arrest her and put some of the stuff in a smaller bag?"

"An ounce like you said. Then we were going to book her for possession."

"So where is the rest of the bag?"

"Pawn Man we don't know. No one touched the box before Mitchell opened it during the search. I put the bag in the damn box myself!"

"That was a mega dime bag!"

"Mega Dime?"

"That stuff was worth a thousand dollars on the streets of this village."

Officer Sherwood didn't like the look in the Pawn man's eyes.

CHAPTER THIRTYFOUR

Quantum Theory

Benjamin sat on his bed. Josh lounged on the floor. Mikey walked down the stairway from the secret room and flopped on the bed.

"What did he she or it say?" Benjamin asked.

"We need to give that computer a name Benjamin."

"If anyone can come up with one you can Mikey."

"Josh. You say there isn't a problem it can't solve?"

"You tested it didn't you?"

"In a way I was sizing the situation up, sort of."

"Is this some bullshit from you Mikey." Josh asked.

"What did you ask it?" Benjamin wanted to know.

"I asked it why it was up here screwing around with you two."

"I wonder what Quantum said to that question?" Benjamin asked, looking at Josh.

"It asked me where here was."

"And what did you tell Quantum?"

"I said that I didn't have a clue."

"That was a big mistake Mikey." Josh told him.

"Why?"

"The one thing we learned, so far, about the Quantum Computer is that it stores all of the known information in the universe."

"So?"

"Quantum is busy right now looking for a clue."

"Did I give Quantum the wrong answer?" Mikey asked'

"Quantum does not know what it is not to know." Josh told his brother.

"Then I must explain what I meant." Mikey told them.

"To Quantum there are no wrong answers, only incorrect questions." Benjamin told him.

"That is the reason we must use the door to the room. The reason we can carry objects in our dimension which others don't see, allows us the ability to be here in another dimension. In the next dimension we understand that things simply are, that time is the same thing as space.*

"Sure Benjamin. Tomorrow morning my Tudor will meet me above the police station. They expelled me from school. They think I'm a psycho cause you two want to space out. You guys are the crazy ones."

Josh grabbed his brother and threw him on the bed laughing. "While you are being taught math above the chief's office, Ben and I put the bag of dope in Officer Sherwood's locker in the squad room. Now he has to explain how the bag of dope ended up in his locker once the Chief reads the E-Mail we put in his computer."

"Sherwood will find a way to blame us." Mikey told them. It is time for a smoke in the gatekeeper's room."

Benjamin and Josh started to go downstairs to talk to Ben's mother.

"Close the door to the room Mikey." Benjamin told him. "Josh and I are going to see if we can talk mom into keeping you here."

"Here? Where is here Ben?"

"So what did you tell the computer Mikey when it asked you where here was?" What was your answer?"

"I told Quantum that here is wherever my dick goes."

"Did it agree with you Mikey?"

"It asked me to come again, in other words guys to repeat."

"Josh and Benjamin giggled their way down the stairs to the kitchen.

Father Edward

The priest sat in his room. His mind circled around the events of the day.

This was the third parish the bishop had placed him to perform his secular

duties. Father Edward decided to go to Benjamin's home. He needed closure

for his behavior just as his confessionals absolved those who asked for his

forgiveness.

Mrs. Winslow would see what a disturbed son she was trying to raise.

She would allow the Priest to commit Benjamin to the detention center. It was

the only way she could save her son and rehabilitate the boy.

The kitchen in Benjamin's house was to be a busy place that night.

Benjamin and Josh Arrive

The boy's entered the kitchen. Benjamin's mom hugged him.

"Mom you're hurting me!"

Josh ate a cookie.

"Where is Mikey?" Benjamin's mother asked.

"He is taking a bath mom." Benjamin replied. "He can't be here when

Officer Sherwood arrives."

"So let me get this straight." Josh said. "Father Edward and Officer Sherwood are coming over here to talk to you Mrs. Winslow?"

"Yes Josh and Mrs. Fontana will stay here as a witness."

"I wouldn't miss it for all the policemen in China" Mrs. Fontana laughed.

Benjamin put his arms around her and hugged the lady who had been looking out for him since they moved into her house.

"You know what all this about don't you?" Benjamin asked, being careful not to squeeze her like his mom did to him.

"I'm ready to hear what both Officer Sherwood and Father Edward have to say." She answered.

Keeping the Gatekeeper

Officer Sherwood sat next to the priest. "This won't take long." He said to the group.

"You called me officer to discuss a problem you are having with my son and his friends." Benjamin's mother began.

"They have claimed that Father Edward sexually molested them. You know how this can ruin the reputation of any person even though the accusations are not true?"

"These attempts to destroy me are most heinous!"

"Your son needs help Mrs. Winslow. There are experienced counselors in the county juvenile center." Father Edward told her.

"Is that what you did to Josh Father? You had him jailed because he was exposing you for sexually attacking him?"

"Josh made up all those stories." Father Edward told her.

"The ladies in the Rosary Society tell me that Josh injured you Father." Mrs. Fontana said to him.

Father Edward turned pale.

"He did injure me by biting me with his teeth."

"How else would I bite you Father?" Josh asked the priest.

"Where did he bite you Father?" Mrs. Fontana asked.

"That is privileged information. Josh is a juvenile and his records are sealed.

"So that's how you got away with it!" Josh cried.

Josh and Benjamin laughed.

Father Edward started to speak. Officer Sherwood raised his hand and silenced him.

Officer Sherwood pointed his finger to Mrs. Fontana.

"What is she doing here? She has nothing to do with this."

"Are you forgetting where you are officer? This is my house. I agreed to meet with you and the Father to discuss what is going on. It involves all of us."

Officer Sherwood stood up and glared at Josh.

"Your brother and his classmates made a fool of me!"

"That's not very hard to do sir."

"You and your friend here were in on it were you not?"

"Not." Josh told him.

"Mrs. Winslow. Your son needs serious help. We can help him if you let us." Father Edward told her.

"Let you do what Father?"

"They have special education programs."

"Father Edward. You are not in any position to help anyone. You need help yourself." Mrs. Fontana told him.

"Who are you old lady to decide what the Father needs or doesn't need?" Officer Sherwood asked her.

Benjamin stood behind his mother.

"Mom, we agreed to meet with you tonight along with Father Edward and Officer Sherwood. You have my word that neither Josh nor I have done anything wrong. That includes Mikey."

"I believe you Benjamin after what has happened."

"Good for you mother of Benjamin!" Mrs. Fontana cried.

"It doesn't matter." Officer Sherwood told them. "We are not the ones who will decide. It is up to our judicial system and Judge Wolfe has directed me to take both of these boys in for questioning."

Officer Sherwood smiled. He placed his hand on the holster holding his new gun.

"Benjamin, you and Josh are both under arrest. Come with me."

Father Edward walked to the kitchen door. "Do what the officer says boys."

CHAPTER THIRTYFIVE

The Rosary Society

Mrs. Fontana blocked their way at the kitchen door.

"Father Edward. May I have a word with you, a moment please?"

"Mrs. Fontana, you are interfering with a police matter here." Father Edward told her.

"An obstruction of justice is a serious crime lady. It could even be a felony Mrs. Fontana." Officer Sherwood told her.

"Gentlemen please. Why are you treating these young boys like this, taking them from their mothers?"

"You need to stay out of this Mrs. Fontana." Father Edward said.

"Why Father? Didn't you have a mother? What about our blessed Mother, the Virgin Mary?" She asked.

"What has the Virgin Mary got to do with these village street irregulars?" Father asked her. "You have heard of the separation of the Church and the State?"

"Yes Father. I know about that." She told him.

"You know what these boys have done to destroy the credibility of our church?"

Mrs. Fontana touched the Father's hand. "You talk about destroying the credibility of our church Father? Our Rosary Society has prayed for you since you came to our church. We have heard many stories Father. Our members talk about you, but they are afraid to speak against the things you have done to these boys. You think you are forgiven by one of our sacred sacraments. Our Bishops keep moving you from one parish to another. You sexually abuse our children believing not only that God will forgive you but that the boys will forget and forgive you as well. Children often do that when they are helpless and afraid."

Father Edward crossed himself as he spoke to Benjamin's mother.

"Your son has accused me of sexually abusing him Mrs. Winslow. We need to place him in a home where people can help him get through his fantasies."

"Our Society will not let you do this to an innocent child Father. If you and Officer Sherwood do not walk out of this room right now, leaving these boys alone, there will be no end of prayer's against your evil ways." Mrs. Fontana told

him.

"Your Rosary Society is a group of senile old women. "You sit hour after

hour praying before the Monstrance." Father Edward told her.

"The Monstrance, what is that?" Josh asked. Mrs. Fontana smiled as she

placed her hands on Josh's shoulders.

"The Monstrance is the body of Christ Josh. Remember, he was placed

upon the cross and died at the hands of the Roman Policemen."

Father Edwards cried. "They were the soldiers of Rome! They were not

policemen!"

"This has gone too far!" Sherwood told them. "We can all go down to the

station now or I can call for backup."

"Did you say call for more backbone?" Josh asked.

"That's it! Either you boys get out of here and get into the car downstairs

or the county deputies will be here!"

"Will they have enough cars to take us?" Mrs. Fontana asked him.

Father Edward cried. "They're gone." He said.

"Who's gone?" Sherwood asked.

"The Boys are gone. While you were standing here arguing, they vanished.

"They have to be here!" Sherwood ran to the stairs almost falling as he climbed them.

"Oh my, they are gone." Mrs. Fontana cried. "I wonder where they are. They were here a minute ago."

CHAPTER THIRTYSIX

Sherwood Cages the Gate Keeper

"Where are they you little piece of crap?"

"Is my mother here yet?" Mikey asked.

Sherwood scratched his head. He tried to figure out how to go about getting the information from this boy.

"You know where they are!" Sherwood realized he needed to calm down. It wasn't going to be easy.

"Where who are where you say I know where they are." The boy replied.

Sherwood kicked the chair Mikey sat in. He was thrown to the floor as the chair fell on top of him.

 Benjamin's mother opened the door of the interrogation room, stopping suddenly.

"Get out of here!" Sherwood shouted. "You have no right to be in here."

Mrs. Fontana brushed past Ben's mother and took the chair off of Mikey. "This has gone far enough. His mother is not here!"

Officer Mitchell entered the room. "What the hell is going on with these women coming into the police station?" He cried.

The two police officers locked Mrs. Winslow, Mrs. Fontana and Mikey in the cage.

"How did you find your way down here below our squad room?" Officer Mitchel asked.

"It's a place known for what happened here a few years ago." Mrs. Fontana replied.

"Then you both better leave here. We have Mikey under arrest."

"You can't do this to us." Mrs. Fontana said.

"You are obstructing justice lady. Yes we can."

"Don't you call me a lady you poor excuse of a man! What you are doing is not justice. When this is over you will be run out of this town on a log, tarred and feathered!"

"Where the hell did she come from Sherwood? Mitchell asked.

"Don't worry about her Mitch. Father Edward will handle her."

"Who is going to handle Father Edward?" Mrs. Fontana asked, very loudly.

Officer Mitchell groaned. "We have to get these women out of here. What is the boy charged with?"

"Obstruction of justice I guess."

Mitchell opened the cage. "You girls come with me." He said.

He walked the ladies to their car. "You have no right to be here. The boy is not your son."

Mitchell followed them home. "Everything will be fine." He said.

Mrs. Fontana stood next to the police car.

"What are you going to do to Mikey?"

"We will turn him over to the judge in the morning. The judge will call the boy's attorney."

"What about tonight? Does he have to stay in that cage?"

"No problem ladies. Lt. Frank comes on duty at midnight. He will take good care of the boy."

They walked into the house not quite believing Officer Mitchell.

'We will be there in the morning." Mrs. Fontana called after him as he drove away in the squad car.

Midnight: The Cage

Lt. Frank sat at the desk outside of the cage.

"There isn't any blanket or pillow here." Mikey told him.

"We don't want you to hang yourself."

"You didn't feed me dinner."

"We don't serve dinner after midnight."

"So what's for breakfast then?" Mikey asked.

"Sherwood said you were a clown."

"Sherwood said you were gay." Mickey told the night officer.

"How did you get that bruise above your eye?" The Lt. asked him.

"You were the cop on duty the night that kid was hanged, weren't you?" Mikey asked.

"The night the boy hanged himself you mean?"

"No. I meant what I said. He was hanged. He didn't hang himself."

"Just like your broken arm? You really shouldn't have tried to climb to the top of the cage. Nasty fall you had there." The Lt. sneered.

"Had?"

"In the morning it will be the past tense."

"Benjamin said this was an evil village."

"Benjamin?"

"He is a friend of ours, me and my brother's friend."

"Didn't your brother Josh attack the priest? He was lucky to get out of this cage alive. Father Edward wanted him in the detention center so we had to let him go."

"Guess you are not a nice man then?"

"Good guess. Now before my first break," Lt. Frank laughed, "It is time for your first break."

"You mean my arm?"

"Boys like you are always breaking their arms in jail."

The Lt. took his key from the desk and walked over to the cage. When he tried to put it into the lock the key fell from his hand.

"Butter Fingers to you!" Mikey said.

As Lt. Frank bent over to retrieve the key he was knocked onto the floor. The key lifted into the air and was inserted into the cage door.

"What took you faggots so long?" Mikey asked. "I could have been in the same cell with Frankenstein here."

"We had to make sure Mikey. This is the man who killed Patrick last year."

"All Pat did was ride a bike home from a party. He just took the wrong bike. Damn!"

"And he ended up in this cell with this monster."

"They had no proof that it wasn't suicide." Mikey said.

"What about tonight? He was going to break my arm."

"But not hang you Mikey."

"Sheeezzzz! Let's get the hell out of here you hero's"

"Hero's?"

"Sorry. You hero faggots!"

CHAPTER THIRTYSEVEN

Home Again

Benjamin's mother was not pleased when they walked into the kitchen.

"Mrs. Fontana is taking this better than I ever could."

"She has faith in us." Mikey told her.

"She needs to talk to the computer." Josh said.

"No. No computers. You boys play enough games on the computer. Just let me stay computer unfriendly. I don't want to know about your games especially if your Grandfather is involved."

"So you will let us keep on playing this game we are playing Mom?" Benjamin asked.

"Benjamin. All I have ever wanted to do is protect you. Now it seems you are protecting me."

"Grandfather has protected us mom. Remember how we got here?"

"He gave me a choice Benjamin. Live here in this God forsaken place or in the mountains of Oregon."

"Why did you pick here Mom?"

"This is where my family is."

"When is the last time you saw Uncle Rodger Mom?"

"Benjamin. We can go anywhere you want to go to."

"What do you think about going to the moon mom?"

"Anywhere Benjamin, as long as you are there, and there are no Officer Sherwood's or Father Edwards around."

"You really ought to think twice about that Mrs. Thompson. Your son is really weird." Mikey said.

"But not as weird as you Mikey. You need to talk to Quantum, now." Benjamin said.

"Quantum, who is this Quantum and what does he do?" Benjamin's mother asked.

"It's just another computer game Mrs. Winslow." Josh assured her.

"I am going into my room. You boys just go upstairs. It is three o'clock in the morning! How you got Mikey out of that police station is not something I want to know. When the phone rings in the morning we will see how bad things look."

Mikey started singing. "A bowl of oatmeal starred me down and won!"

"Common Mikey you have a Gate to keep." Josh told him.

"But I didn't kill anyone. Just trying to have me some fun!"*

"That's enough Mikey." His rescuers chased him up the stairs.

Mikey Thanks Quantum

That night Josh introduced Mikey to Quantum Computer. "He is my brother."

Mikey stood in front of the large monitor screen. Quantum replayed the rescue scene in the cage. Lt. Frank was now locked inside the cage standing on a chair. His hands were tied behind him and a noose was placed around his neck. The rope from the noose was securely fastened to the top of the cage. Unfortunately for the lieutenant the room was soundproof and it did no good to call for help.

"Guess Lieutenant Frank has a long night until they come to get me in the morning." Mikey said. "Thank you Quantum for saving me." Mikey smiled at the computer.

"You're welcome. Nobody messes with my gatekeeper." Quantum told him.

"Do you think the police will be over here after they discover the lieutenant in the cage."

"No doubt in my quantum mind."

"What are we going to do?" Mikey asked.

"Benjamin and Josh will spend the night with me. You go down to the bathroom and close the door to our room."

"Won't they take me back to the cage and finish what they were going to do to me?"

"Not if they can't see you Mikey." Josh told him. You are in the fourth dimension now."

"Have a good night brother." Josh said. "We will see you after they raid the place."

"You can sleep in my bed." Benjamin said.

CHAPTER THIRTYEIGHT

Speed of Light

"We are moving at the speed of light in another universe but in this one we are traveling in a circle at a slower speed."

Benjamin entered this information in his Star Map Log.

"What is the difference between a dimension and a universe?" Josh asked.

"Depends on which direction you are traveling." Quantum answered. "You have told us that light waves can move forward and backward. The new calculus proves that it is possible to halt the speed of light." Josh explained.

Quantum hummed and clicked. "A universe has dimensions depending on the speed you travel. The dimensions are inside a universe. If you suspend yourself on the edge of a black hole, time would stop. Time is space times the speed of light. Moving at the speed of light you can measure dimension. When you move faster than the speed of light you are moving into the future."

Josh shrugged. Then if you are moving slower than the speed of light you are traveling back into the past?"

"The movement of the dimension along with the all of its particles it is composed of, as physicists like to call them, is the micro-cosmos. If you move away from one dimension toward another, inside the universe, it is called the macro-cosmos."

"How can we ever travel at the speed of light?" Benjamin asked.

"Only light travels at the speed of light." The Quantum Machine told them.

"We cannot travel at the speed of light then?" Josh asked.

"There is a way for you to travel at the speed of light." Quantum said.

"What laws do we have to break in order to do it?" Benjamin asked.

"You have up to this point broken two of those laws." Quantum reminded them.

"Which law do we need to overcome to travel at the speed of light?" Josh asked.

"Overcome?" Quantum asked.

"Yes. It sounds better to overcome a law rather than to break it." Benjamin said.

"It looks like we have broken enough laws in the third dimension to be put away for the rest of eternity." Josh told the Computer.

"Quantum, you don't mind if we call you Quantum, do you?" Benjamin asked.

"No offense taken. My instinct tells me my new name came from the Gate Keeper."

"Instinct, you have intuition, instinct and the ability to know the meaning of human jest?" Josh asked.

Since meeting Mikey different changes have occurred in my programs. I'm processing them in order to communicate intelligently." Quantum replied.

"That is what Mikey is, a jester." Josh told Quantum.

"That is a new word, jester, but it will make sense, like my name, once I search my files."

"The Gate Keeper clowns around a lot Quantum." Josh said.

"Wait a mega second. OH! He is a star circling inside a cosmic dust storm? NO. He is a humorous person who entertains a king. I must speak to him in order to find out why he gives me the name Quantum when we met only one time."

"That's all it takes with Mikey." Josh said. "He has one word to describe everyone he knows."

"He can really piss people off Quantum." Benjamin said.

"Piss people off Josh? Is that an idiom in your language?"

"Yes. Piss." Josh said.

"A slang word for urine ejected from the human body by way of the urinary system." Quantum hummed. "It means that Mikey urinates on people."

Benjamin. Are you sure Grandfather said the Quantum Computer has all of the third dimensional information?"

Quantum hummed. "I found it! Piss people off. It is a euphemism for 'Irritate another person', right?"

"That didn't take long," Benjamin said, "Your processors are quick."

"I'm only a first generation machine. They sent me here to train you, not to play twenty questions."

"Mikey needs to spend more time with you Quantum. A couple of hours with him and you will be up to speed on the…what did you say that word was?"

"Euphemisms Josh, a blunt expression spoken instead of a polite one."

"Not a calculus word Ben."

"It isn't on any of my map charts Josh."

CHAPTER THIRTYNINE

The Church

The Church Council met in the rectory office. Twelve members gathered around the table waiting for the Pastor. Mrs. Fontana represented the Rosary Society. She sat across from Father Edward and Attorney Gerald.

The pastor entered the room. They all stood out of respect for the head Priest. He motioned for them to be seated.

The Father blessed the members following the opening prayer.

"The first item on our agenda concerns the recent problems in our elementary school program. My assistant pastor, Father Edward, prepared a report for us following an extensive investigation which he conducted with the teachers, students and the school employees. Father Edward will now give us a summary of his findings."

Father Edward nodded. "You all know about the rumors and the stories that are being spread within the church community. Three students have joined together to disrupt the educational program. They are questioning the teachings of the church. One of them has accused me of sexually molesting him. In my report you will find statements from the faculty and the school employees

supporting my findings."

"Have you interviewed the three students involved?" The Church Attorney

asked?

"They have run away. The police are looking for them as we speak."

"Did you sexually molest the boy accusing you Father? Mrs. Fontana

asked the priest.

"Mrs. Fontana, with all due respect you are out of order. No one called

upon you to speak!" The Pastor told her.

Mrs. Fontana stood up and addressed the church council. "The Rosary

Society calls for Father Edward's resignation." She told them. "Father Edward

is a disgrace not only to this church but to this community."

"You may speak for the Rosary Society Mrs. Fontana but in this meeting

you cannot speak for our community. You are out of order!" Attorney Gerald

cried.

"Then the members of the Rosary Society call for the resignation of Father

Edward." Mrs. Fontana said."

"You cannot enter a call in this meeting Mrs. Fontana. You are totally out of order." The Pastor told her.

"Seems to me this whole church is out or order!" She said.

"We must ask you to leave the meeting now Mrs. Fontana." The Pastor told her.

"None of you will discuss the creation of a prison mission! You won't open the Elementary School and offer programs and activities that keep the children off the streets! The members of this church only want to serve Christ inside its brick walls! If Jesus walked into this meeting right now, you would call 911 and have him arrested."

The council members were silent.

"This meeting is adjourned!" The Pastor ordered.

"Not by a majority vote it isn't." Mrs. Fontana said.

The Pastor's Study

Attorney Gerald motioned to the Pastor and Father Edward. They left the meeting and the three of them entered the Pastor's office.

Closing the door, to the Pastor's office, the attorney put his hand on Father Edward's shoulder. "Pack your bags Father. You are leaving the village as soon as possible."

"That old witch can't do this to me! You are the church's attorney. This is preposterous!"

"If you have been true to your vows Father you will not have too many things to pack."

"Where will I go?" Father Edward asked.

"The Bishop of Rochester has a room for you in the rehab center for priests."

"Rehabilitation is not what I need. What I need is sympathy and understanding."

"Just stay away from little old ladies Father."

"Why?"

"They protect little girls and boys."

"Protect them from me?"

"From Priests who give a vow of chastity, then seduce young boys to satisfy their sexual urges Father."

"Priests offer these children love?" the Father tried to explain.

"Protecting the innocent children from predators like you, children whose parents no longer accept the animal instinct to protect their young." The attorney explained.

"What I did to those boys was the Love Christ taught us. I tried to be the father they never had."

"You were having sexual affairs with them, especially against their will?"

"Sex is a great gift from God."

"You were the pastor in the detention center. You gave them special privileges in exchange for sex with them."

"They got what they wanted for what I wanted, God's Love."

"Love Father Edward?"

"The boys never said no."

"Is that why one of them bit you on your hard love shaft Father?" The Pastor asked.

"He was a disturbed boy."

"The Pastor has arranged for a member of the church to drive you to Rochester."

"Will it happen tonight?"

"The sooner it happens, the better for everyone concerned." The attorney told him.

"The church will stand by me. Their lawyer in Rochester will be in touch with you."

"He better be a damn good one Father."

Village Court

Judge Wolfe entered his office located next to the courtroom.

Attorney Gerald was sitting in a chair with his head bowed. He was confused. He represented the District Attorney's office for the County. The agenda at St. James Church was thrown to the wind.

Judge Wolfe put his robe on.

"You have any idea what's going on here Counselor?"

"We sent the priest to Rochester. He is on the way to the Bishop's Rectory."

"Do you have the charges against the boys written up?"

The Attorney handed the documents to the judge. "Ready for your signatures your honor including the warrants."

"What do I do now?" The magistrate asked. "What are the charges?"

"There are many, including Felony escape from a jail cell; Obstruction of justice; Refusal to obey a Police Officer."

"Is everyone in the courtroom?"

"Yes, including their attorney Mrs. Fontana."

"She has legal proof she can practice in this state?"

"She is registered. That woman is amazing. She can be a problem if we want to stay in power."

"Do you think she will run against me in the next election?"

"It wouldn't be a problem if she did. The people in this village are never organized when it comes to politics. There are 2,000 registered voters in the village and only about 600 of them show up at the polls during a presidential election year, otherwise it is rare for a turnout of 320 during local elections."

"What if someone comes in and rally's them to vote for a better village?"

"Then we do what we always do. We get rid of them."

"Like the man in the Bookstore?"

"Judge, if you want a job next year, rid this village of those boys, and the people who support them."

"A good lawyer could see though all of our illegal moves Counselor.

Two things are on our side judge. You were a state policeman. The Federal War on Drugs suspended so many constitutional rights that it takes a good lawyer to figure out what's going on. Second, the people we are dealing with don't have the money to pay a good lawyer."

"We have public defenders for those who can't afford an attorney Counselor."

"In this county we own the public defenders."

"You mean lawyers who have other interests?" The judge laughed.

Attorney Gerard joined in the laughter. "The people we prosecute in this court are not only poor your honor, they are stupid."

"Who said crime doesn't pay?"

The Judge

The Judge banged his gavel. "This court is in session. "Michael Price age twelve a minor, is charged with Felony escape from the Officers of this court."

Mrs. Fontana and Mikey stood up.

"How do you plead?" The judge asked.

"Not guilty." Mrs. Fontana replied.

"As to obstruction of justice on the Part of Benjamin Winslow and Josh Stone, how do the defendant's plead?"

"Not guilty.

"You are to be remanded to the county detention center until such time, set for the hearing, in all cases, two weeks from this date."

"Your honor," Mrs. Fontana said, rising, "This is only an appearance. These boys are not going anywhere. We request they be placed in the custody of their mother."

"Judge," Attorney Gerald said. "The boys have been known to disappear when the Village Police were looking for them. They are a flight risk. They need to be locked up without bail."

"Considering what the boys have done to the officers of this court Mrs. Fontana, they are not to be trusted in the care of their guardians." The Judge said.

"Then put them in my care your honor. As an officer of the court, I can assure you that they will appear at any hearing."

Attorney Gerald asked to speak to the Judge in his office.

"Not without me you don't." Mrs. Fontana told them.

"Then step up here." The Judge told them.

They stood together in front of the judge.

Judge Wolfe thought about his cigar and the glass of brandy waiting for him at home.

"In the case of Michael Price, the hearing is set for next Tuesday December 4th. The hearing for Benjamin Winslow, who will appear with Josh Stone, is set for the same time."

"Who will have custody of the boys' your honor?" The Prosecuting attorney asked.

"Let Mrs. Fontana take them with her. If they are as bad as you say Counselor than she deserves to have them until next Tuesday."

"May I remind you your honor that these boys are able to vanish into thin air."

"Then why are they here in this courtroom Counselor?"

CHAPTER FORTY

Sherwood and Mitchell

"These donuts are yesterdays." Mitchell said.

"It is three in the morning." Sherwood told him. "It could be that they were made today and you think it is yesterday."

"How the hell did you ever get to be a policeman?" Mitchell asked.

"My father helped me. He had some favors owed to him for what he did for the Chief."

"You mean the boy hanging in the village jail?"

"They were going to hang Lieutenant Frank for that incident but I was there."

"Hang?"

"You know what I mean."

"The boy did steal the bicycle didn't he?

"Not really. He just took the wrong bike."

"So why didn't someone come to the station and take the boy home?"

"I called the boy's father. When I explained that his son was in the police station he hung up on me."

"How did you know it was the boy's father?"

"Before he hung up he told me to keep him in jail. He said his son was the reason for all his problems that the boy was going to testify against him in the county court the next day."

"What?"

"The man I talked to on the phone?"

"It was Lieutenant Frank."

"You mean the boy who hung himself in the cell that night was Frank's son?"

"No Sherwood. He was the son of Lieutenant Frank's girlfriend."

Night Patrol

Officer Sherwood parked on a lonely stretch of road below the country club. It was time for the bars to close. The club members would be driving down the hill to the village heading home to sleep off the night of drink and dancing.

Some of them would have sweet dreams. The women would not be so fortunate. Officer Sherwood chose the cars with females and stopped them before they reached the traffic light at the bottom of the hill.

The ladies had two choices. They could blow into the Breathalyzer tube or have sex with Officer Sherwood.

Officer Sherwood stopped one of the vehicles as it drove past him.

Mitchell sat in the police station waiting for Sherwood to return. He did not want to know what his partner did at the end of the late shift. The graveyard was a dull shift. Mitchell dozed and was startled when opened his eyes. Sherwood had not returned from his country club cruise.

The phone on the dispatcher's desk was ringing.

"Mitchell here, what's up?"

"This is the county dispatcher. I got a call from someone driving on Route 23 below the Country Club. He said Officer Sherwood is hand cuffed to the outside of his patrol car."

"This is a joke right?" Officer Mitchell asked.

"Is this you Mitch?" The county dispatcher asked.

"Yeah, who else would work this stinking shift?"

"Officer Sherwood has a slight problem. Someone cuffed him to his car."

"Oh Man!"

Galaxies

Grandfather waited in the room with Quantum. He watched as Benjamin and Josh rode their bikes through the park to the Bookstore. They leaned the bikes against the wall of the store.

"When mom gets home tonight we have to explain what's going on." Benjamin said.

"She can't know about the room." Josh told him.

"What will we tell her?"

"Will she hear us if she can't see us?" Josh asked.

"We have to figure out how to get back into the third dimension Josh."

"The Bookman is in on this Ben. Let's go in and ask him."

"Did you bring the bag?"

"Sure did. It's in my back pack." Josh replied, as he took it from his bike.

"What are we going to do with it?"

"He will tell us Ben.

"Maybe we can sell it to Eric."

"How," Josh asked, "we are invisible?"

"When we find out how to appear again, I guess." Benjamin said.

A car pulled up to the curb where they were standing. "Can you boys tell me where to find the Moose Hall?" The driver asked.

They looked at each other. "Sure. Two blocks up this street." Josh directed him.

Josh! We have to get off the street before Sherwood comes by in his car." Benjamin whispered. "We got this stuff on us."

Entering the side door of the Bookstore, they looked around for the Bookman. He was in the cyber room working on the computer.

Josh walked up to the Bookman. "Is this a quantum machine?" He asked.

The Bookman stood up and laughed. "What brings you guys here at this hour?"

"This." Benjamin told him holding up the bag of marijuana.

"Ah well now this is a serious matter."

"Officer Sherwood tried to plant this on my mom." Benjamin told him.

"Then we need to teach this Sherwood a lesson."

"But how can we do that?" Benjamin asked.

"Put it in his locker at the police station. Then, when he is off duty in the morning, call the Chief on your cell phone. Tell him you are wondering when the officer will pay you for the bag of marijuana that you put in his locker last night.

Tell him you are waiting in the Donut Shop for the money."

"The Chief is going to believe this?"

"Yes, if you tell him you left the bag in his locker. Say you are the boy

arrested last night by Officer Sherwood but he let you escape when you put the

bag in his locker."

"But it would be a lie." Benjamin told the Bookman.

"The same lie Sherwood would have used to put your mother in jail."

"How are we going to get into the locker room? Josh asked. "Someone in

a car saw us outside before we came in here."

"That was the Mountain Man."

"He didn't have a beard." Benjamin said.

"You don't either Benjamin."

What is he doing here tonight? I thought he was back in Oregon in his

observatory?"

He was cruising below the Country Club, on the hill, where Office

Sherwood likes to finish his shift." The Bookman answered.

Josh pulled Benjamin outside of the store onto the sidewalk.

"Let's do this thing he told us to do and get back home Ben before Officer Sherwood finds us."

"Somehow I feel Sherwood is a little hung up Josh."

"What will we say to your mom Ben?"

"That space and time are a drag."

"That's very funny Einstein, coming from you."

CHAPTER FOURTYONE

Systems Analysis

Martin turned on his computer. His bedroom was comfortable. Fortunately his father allowed him to have a computer that connected to another world. Martin knew his father didn't accept the world outside of his church.

If only his mother could be here. Then Martin's world would be like it was before.

Einstein was correct. The gravity of his room was a heavy weight. His room was a space and a time where his father punished him. Martin knew about time and space in a child's world.

The adults tricked you into thinking how the future should be lived if you believed what they taught you. Martin was forced to listen to the teachings in the church. Fine with him except you were not supposed to question them.

"Guess Einstein's parents weren't like that." Martin thought.

His computer beeped, waking him from his daydream.

When Martin asked his father uncomfortable questions he was sent his room. Martin learned something very important when he reached others, who taught him the language of mathematics on the internet.

"Don't ask me these questions. Go to your room and ask yourself how God can help you. Pray to him Martin. Pray and God will answer," His father would say sending him to his room.

"Yes Father."

When he was twelve years old, Martin learned that if you have a computer and a modem connected to a phone line, you are communicating with the creator of the universe.

Sunflower.Com

Martin met his friend Penny in school. He thought she was the most beautiful girl he had ever seen.

When he told her about his father and all the hours he was forced to spend alone in his room, Penny sat next to him under one of the trees in the school yard.

"Your mom died when you were born. What do you expect from a preacher? My mother says he believes God is punishing him every day." Penny said.

"Penny!"

"Martin?"

"What are you doing this summer?" Martin asked her.

"Mom is sending me to my Grandfather's farm in Oregon.

"He has this huge barn and a silo. We fish and swim and hike and grow things."

"Don't you get bored?" Martin asked.

"My grandfather has other children living there. We learn about astronomy and math."

"Learning, what fun is that?"

"Learning is fun Martin," Penny told him, "especially when it makes your life better. Tell me one thing Martin. When you learn something you enjoy and it is fun to learn don't you feel great about it?"

"Yes!"

Penny was pleased to take his thoughts away from his father.

Martin thought for several moments.

"Here is what you do Martin. Tonight log on to your computer and search for Sunflower.Com."

"What if my father comes in and sees the chat room?"

"Martin. Tonight your father will be with my mother in the church basement."

"But it's not choir night." He told her.

Martin could not figure out what Penny was talking about. She was such a beautiful person and really understood how he felt about his father. She understood what he talked about in math class. She was not only beautiful but she was smart. Most girls seemed to hide their intelligence and he could never figure out why.

"How many kids are at the farm?" He asked.

"Oh we just come and go Martin. Check it out on the address I gave you."

"Why should I?" Martin asked her.

"You like calculus Martin?"

"Calculus, Penny, I am a calculus machine. If my father knew about all of the hours that I spent in my room learning calculus and theoretical calculus he would be very angry. I was supposed to be praying to God. My computer would have been history. My searches took me to a site at Princeton University. The graduate students called me the Calculus Kid.

"Why did they do that Martin?"

"OK. The students started playing games with me. They tested me. It took some before I was able to convince them that my questions were serious, that I wasn't just some nerd kid in some high school playing games with them. They chatted with me every night. I was so happy to be in the same room with them."

"Did they know you were twelve years old" Penny asked.

"No Penny. I figured that if they knew they were teaching math to a kid they would knock me off line."

"Wow Martin! The mathematical formulas must have been so exciting. How did you get into their space?"

"My father gave me the computer."

"Martin! Your father has no idea what's going on in cyberspace."

"That is very true Penny. My father kind of felt guilty about not spending time with me. That's how I got the computer and all the devices."

"Adults are so confusing." Penny cried. "Martin. When you get in your room tonight, go to Sunflower.Com. They will ask you for the pass word."

"What is it Penny?"

"Type in and enter 'Morning Glory'."

CHAPTER FORTYTWO

Time Travel

Martin shared his loneliness with the trees surrounding him. His father sent him to the camp with the hope that Martin would find the real world.

The lake was clear and clean. The camp counselors sang in the mess hall where the meals were served.

Martin knew that he was a prisoner in the camp. In two weeks he would return to another prison, his bedroom. Martin's father was a Lutheran Minister with a small parish in northern Pennsylvania.

Martin finished his oatmeal and was about to throw his burnt toast away when a new camp counselor called for their attention.

"A morning song for you guys. We don't usually sing after breakfast but the director agreed to let me teach you this one."

"Good Morning, Morning glory, Good morning Good morning to you. Good Morning, Morning glory, good morning, good morning to you."

Martin felt as though the dining hall turned into another place.

WELCOME TO CAMP
LUTHER
ARCHERY   10:00 AM
RIFLE RANGE NOON
ANIMAL STALKING
3:00 NORTH LAKE
DRESSING A DEER
4:00 CAMP BARN
TRAPPING BEAVER
6:00 SOUTHPOND

When they were dismissed Martin walked down to the lake.

The counselor who sang the song walked past him.

"Welcome to the world Martin."

Martin smiled. "I always knew there was another world out here." He said.

"Sometimes you have to be in a prison in order to see what real freedom is."

The counselor told him.

Martin jumped up and ran across the field in front of the dining hall.

Someone shouted at him. "There is no running in this camp!"

Martin disappeared into the woods. "Good morning, good morning glory!"

He yelped as he went into the trees.

Martin

On the night before he went to camp his father sent him to his room.

"Your principal called today. You argued with your teacher."

"Which one was that Sir?"

"You don't disagree with your teacher or any adult for that matter, Martin."

"She said you can only divide a prime number by itself or 1."

"And you told her she was wrong?"

"No father. I just told her that a prime number is divisible by any number."

"You do not have the right to question your teacher Martin. You know that. I have taught you to not be disrespectful."

"But it is true. I didn't argue with her. I just told the truth."

"You are too young to know the truth Martin. The earth revolves around the sun. The sun does not revolve around you."

"Yes father. I am truly sorry sir."

"In that case Martin, go to your room. Because you are sorry I won't take away your computer privileges."

"Thank you father, you are good to me."

"Are you all packed and ready for camp?"

"Yes sir."

"We will leave right after breakfast so get plenty of rest."

"Yes father. Goodnight."

"At least they don't have computers in this camp." His father told him.

"What will they do there?" Martin asked.

"Teach you to hunt, trap, shoot guns, bows and arrows. Swimming, hunting, fishing; things a boy needs to know in order to get along."

"They teach us how to kill animals?"

"They also teach you to listen and obey orders."

"Whose orders do we learn to obey father?"

"There will always be those who give you orders. They are your superiors. I want you to be ready for the real world son."

"You want me to be a soldier?"

"Yes Martin. You may go to war someday. I want you to be ready."

"What about peace and love father. You talk in church about how we need to love each other as Jesus loved us."

"What do you mean Martin?"

"Father, what about Martin Luther? He nailed the notice on the door of the Roman Church."

"What about Martin Luther Martin? Are you questioning me on theology?"

"He did not accept the teachings of the priests in the Catholic church. He questioned them sir. Was he wrong to do that?"

"Martin Luther was a great theologian. Of course not!"

"Then why can't I ask questions?"

"You are not in the real world yet Martin. When you get there we will discuss how you will deal with the dictates and dogmas of our Church."

"When is that father? When will I be in the real world?"

"Goodnight son."

Martin closed the door to his room.

CHAPTER FORTYTHREE

Grandfather

Mrs. Fontana took her three wards from the courtroom to Benjamin's room.

"Now that you three are members of The Sunflower Council it is time to explain just what it is you boys have gotten yourself into."

"You are a part of all these secret happenings?" Benjamin asked.

"What is the Sunflower Council?" Josh added.

"How are the three of us going to be in the secret room with Quantum if there is no one to be the gate keeper?" Mikey asked.

"Please sit down next to each other over by Benjamin's telescope. I will answer your questions in the order they were asked. Mikey sit on the window seat and keep an eye out for our friends in uniform.

Yes Benjamin. My name is Giana. I have been with the Sunflower Council for a long time. Your grandfather has taken care of us for many years, bringing us together on a project known as the 'Spaceship Sunflower'. We are preparing to travel to the Farm in Oregon. We will leave this village together, traveling to our Farm in Oregon. All of us who have been working on this special project must stay together.

Thus Josh, you are all members of the Sunflower project. The Council is headed by Benjamin's grandfather.

Now Mikey, as to your question, I am the new gatekeeper. You are assigned to Quantum, as you named him, to scout around the village in order to protect your friend Greg and his brother Tommy. Once they are safe in the Secret Room we will transport their mother safely to a hospital, near the farm in Oregon."

"You know about the mother?" Mikey asked.

"Greg's father is a Particle Physicist at Princeton University. He will travel with us on our journey to Oregon."

"So what do we do now?" Mikey asked."

"We go up to the room and meet Grandfather." Benjamin told him.

"What is your Grandfather like Ben?" Mikey Asked.

"You are about to find out for yourself Mikey."

"Describe him in one word man."

"Indescribable?"

"You have to do it Mikey. You have a word for everyone so get ready to meet Grandfather."

Mikey cried as he looked out the window.

"The fuzz has arrived Mrs. Fontana, I mean Giana!"

"We have to get to work boys! Get up there as soon as I turn the handle."

Grandfather Meets Mikey

Grandfather was entering data on the key board as they joined him. Three monitors sat on the desk in front of him. Grandfather turned to face them.

"Well, the space travelers have arrived! Hello Benjamin Josh and Mikey," He smiled, we are in the same place at last!"

"Grandfather!" Benjamin hugged him."We made it here safely."

When Benjamin saw the monitor screens, he laughed. You have a picture of each one of us on the monitors."

"You each have your own stations Benjamin. Now each one of you can go sit in front of the screen opposite your ugly mugs."

Mikey sat in front of his monitor. "Ain't anything ugly about this here kid."

"Quantum is a first generation computer, able to store information at the speed of light."

"When you told me about another dimension Grandfather there was no way for me to know that we would end up in a secret room with a computer like this one."

"The computer at the farm will make Quantum here look like a crank up phone."

"I resent that!" Quantum said.

"Who named this machine Quantum?" Grandfather asked.

"Mikey did. He thought that since it could actually talk to us logically, it deserved to be known by one word, Quantum, instead of Quantum Computer."

"He does this to everyone he meets?" Grandfather asked.

"He sure does." Josh told him.

"Then what do you think he'll call me?" Grandfather asked.

"Mikey would call him Papa." Josh guessed.

"Like they called Hemmingway? Benjamin guessed.

Josh looked at Benjamin. "Ah well, he can, but we thought it was…"

"Maybe Mikey's word for Grandfather is too short!" Benjamin said quickly.

Mikey swiveled his chair from the keyboard. "My word for you is Pops." He told them.

Quantum clicked and hummed. "That will teach you to call me a crank phone." Quantum said.

Grandfather Sneezed and coughed.

"You stay out of this Computer or you can travel to Oregon on a separate train!" Grandfather warned Quantum.

"You would never arrive safely in Portland without me."

"You think you know it all." Grandfather said, as his eye brows raised.

Quantum buzzed and clicked.

"Honestly Quantum!" Grandfather snorted. "You put him up to this."

"You got it Pops!"

"The sun travelers are growing older." Quantum told him. "You may be Benjamin's Grandfather, but his new friends see you in a different light."

Mikey Enters the Fourth Dimension

"Can I go outside and walk around in the fourth dimension Grandfather?" Mikey asked.

"Sure Mikey. We have faith in you." Grandfather told him.

"This should be interesting guys." Mikey said.

Benjamin and Josh shrugged their shoulders.

"What? You think something bad is going to happen?" Mikey asked them.

"No Mikey. Nothing bad, but something is going to happen.

Quantum clicked and hummed.

"Was that your processor Quantum?" Mikey asked. "Never could understand how a computer could make so many gees and haws."

"Clicks and clacks like the printer sounds." Josh added.

Quantum buzzed.

"In case you computer freaks haven't noticed, we make sounds to keep you in touch." Quantum told them.

"Sounds to keep us in touch with what?" Mikey asked Quantum.

Quantum clicked. "You've got mail! In your case Mikey, when you are out there in the fourth dimension you may hear my voice telling you to get your butt back here now."

"How do I do that Quantum?"

"Greg will let you know when. Just save him from Officer Sherwood."

The River

Mikey sat on the rocks under the Interstate Highway Bridge. No one could find him here. He wanted to spend the night alone. It was warm. A tent of logs forming a shelter was built under the trees above the rocks. The river flowed

below him.

Mikey sat listening to the water churning over the stones just as his

thoughts tumbled over what he must do about leaving his mother. She wanted

to go with Eric to North Carolina. Somehow it seemed to Mikey that his life

would not be any different if he went with her. His mother was never going to

change her ways.

Before he entered the Secret Room he wanted to go with them. "You guys

are all really freaked out. Can you just let me out of all this?" He pleaded,

hoping his brother and Benjamin would let him go to North Carolina.

"Where will you go?" Josh asked his brother?"

"Our mother is going to North Carolina with Eric."

"Why is it any better in North Carolina?" Benjamin asked.

"The village police are harassing them. They want to find a place to

smoke their dope in peace." Mikey explained.

"Who will they live with? Will Eric have a job?"

"They don't know."

"So you want to go with them?"

"Someone has to look after her Josh."

"Did you talk about this with Quantum?"

"Yes."

"What does Quantum have to say?" Grandfather asked Mikey.

"Quantum told me that no matter where we go or what we do there is only one way to travel."

"Does that make sense to you?" Grandfather asked.

"Yes Pops."

"What did Quantum say?"

"We need to follow our own heart and travel with those who really love us." Mikey told him.

"How do we know who they are?"

"It is up to our heart to decide." Quantum said. "But heed not these words Mikey, for they are spoken by a foolish Quantum."

"See you at the farm." Mikey said.

Mikey Decides Which Way

"What if the cops get him?" Josh asked.

"Mikey is in the next dimension. No one will see him unless he wants them to see him."

"Mikey?"

"Yes Josh."

"When Mom gets there and she is safe, will you come back here?"

"Won't they be surprised when they drive out of here find me in the back seat of the car somewhere in Maryland?"

"She will talk you into staying with her Mikey." Josh said.

"Mom could talk me into anything before we met Benjamin Josh, but no longer."

"What's so different now Mikey?"

"It is Quantum. Quantum beats me in chess. Quantum has an answer for every question."

"Quantum is a computer Mikey." Josh told his brother. "You never caved in to anyone's opinions before."

"That's just it Josh. Quantum answers my main question. Nobody has ever done that!"

"What question Mikey?"

"The same one I've been asking you for years Josh."

"The question you have been asking me every morning?"

"That's the one!"

CHAPTER FORTYFOUR

Benjamin and Jason

"Where do you suppose Mikey went to tonight?" Benjamin asked.

"He has this spot by the river." Josh said.

"The Rocks where he goes camping," Benjamin asked, "and fishing?"

"You heard about it?"

"Mikey's friend Greg told me. Greg goes there to get away from his mother. When he skipped school, he would sit on the porch but the neighbors would call the police."

"Why?"

"They thought he should be in school."

"So he went to the Rocks when he didn't want to go to school?"

"Why does Greg want to get away from his mother Josh?"

"The same reason your mother left your father Benjamin."

Quantum clicked and hummed. "Want to see Mikey?"

"You can let us see him at the Rocks?"

"We see him in the fourth dimension, yes." Quantum replied.

"Why in the fourth dimension Quantum?"

"That is where Mikey is Josh."

Benjamin sat down in front of his monitor.

"We better keep an eye on Mikey." Josh said. He could get into trouble in any dimension.

Josh looked at Benjamin who looked at Josh.

"How can anything go wrong at the Rocks?" Benjamin asked.

Quantum remained silent for a fraction of a second.

"Can we see Mikey sitting on the rocks, right now?" Josh wondered.

"You are in the room in the fourth dimension. Mikey is in the same dimension as we are." Grandfather explained.

"You can see him sitting on the Rocks. Look at your monitors."

"Those are the Rocks!" Josh cried. "Mikey and I built a fort down there in case Mom had a party night."

"What is a party night?" Quantum asked.

"We'll explain it to you later Quantum." Benjamin told him.

"No need to explain." Quantum said. "It is a party of parties who party?"

"Not bad Quantum. It's a good thing Mikey isn't here to explain what his mother's party of parties did." Josh laughed.

"Of course Josh. That's what people at a party do. They party." Quantum said with a hint of satisfaction.

"Why did Mikey go down to the Rocks?" Benjamin asked Josh.

"I don't know for sure but Mikey and Greg spend a lot of time there. If we wait a few minutes Greg may show up, thinking that Mikey is hiding in our fort. Officer Sherman and Mitchell would never find him there."

CHAPTER FORTYFIVE

Dimensions in One Universe

Mikey knew he was in the fourth dimension. The water passed over the rocks and eddied along the riverbank.

Quantum told me that there were four dimensions in this universe. When I asked him where the next dimension was he told me it was in the next parallel universe. When I asked Quantum why Josh, Benjamin and I couldn't walk through walls he told me that being in the fourth dimension meant we were in the same universe. Light does not travel through walls.   When I asked Quantum where the fifth dimension was, Quantum hummed buzzed and clicked.

Mikey stood up as a car approached the Rocks. It was the village patrol car turning in the cul-de-sac where the dirt road ended above the Rocks.

As Mikey watched, Officer Sherwood and Mitchell got out of the patrol car and opened the back doors.

"Get out!" Sherwood said to the person in the back seat.

"Why did you bring me here?" Someone asked.

"Don't ask!" Mitchell shouted. "Get out of the 'friggin' car."

Mikey's friend Greg stepped onto the grass next to Officer Mitchell.

"This isn't legal." Greg told them. "You have no right to do this to me!"

"Well, well, the boy is a lawyer." Mitchell laughed.

"Take me home!" Greg shouted.

"Where were you going when we picked you up?" Sherwood asked him.

"I was going to the store!"

"Shopping lifting again?"

"I was getting ice cream for my brother. He is waiting for me at home."

"Let him wait." Mitchell said. "At least we got you before you got the ice cream. Now it won't melt."

"You are pigs!"

Sherwood knocked the boy to the ground. The officers dragged him to the edge of the woods.

Mikey ran toward them yelling. "Leave him alone!"

They don't see me or hear me.

Officer Sherwood stood Greg against a tree as Mitchell handcuffed the boy's hands behind the tree.

"No Mitch. Use a rope. When they find him the handcuffs it will give us away."

Mitchell returned to the car and opened the trunk. He took the rope from the car and slammed the lid.

They removed the cuffs and tied the boy's hands behind the tree.

"Let's take off his clothes." Mitchell said. "Remember how you were left naked and cuffed to your patrol car?"

"How about we question him first?" Sherwood said.

"A naked prisoner answers questions faster."

Greg spit in Officer Sherwood's face.

Officer Mitchell started removing the boy's shirt. "Where is your pervert boyfriend?" He asked.

Greg stopped struggling. "People come down here every night." He said.

"We know. They will find you here after we finish with you." Sherwood told him.

"Where are your friends?" Officer Sherwood demanded.

"Which friends are you talking about?"

"We are looking for Mikey and his brother Josh!"

"Down by the Rocks." Greg told them.

"Yes!" Officer Sherwood cried. "We got them."

The Secret Room

Quantum Josh and Benjamin sat quietly in the room when Grandfather left them.

"Want to see Mikey at the Rocks now?" Quantum asked Benjamin and Josh.

Mikey told my Grandfather that he was going down to the rocks to decide if he will go with us to the farm in Oregon or take off for North Carolina with Eric and his mother." Benjamin said.

Josh crossed his fingers. "He won't leave me for her and the streets on North Carolina."

"Anyone taking bets here?" Quantum asked.

"Yes Quantum. Show us my crazy brother. He said he was going to North Carolina in the morning with Mom and Eric." Josh said.

Mikey appeared on all three monitors.

"I told you he was crazy Ben. Mikey is walking around something." Josh said.

"Looks like some kind of dance." Benjamin said.

"Maybe he is practicing Tai Chi." Quantum said.

"Not Mikey! He seems to be doing something to someone in the third dimension. Do you think he is saying goodbye to a friend?"

"He reached into something we can't see. Now he is going around and pushing something, we can't see, down the hill toward the Rocks." Benjamin said.

"He is pushing hard. He is going faster down the hill toward the rocks." Josh said.

The Rocks

"Go down there and get them." Officer Sherwood told Mitchell.

Mitchell disappeared down the hill.

"If they aren't there you little jerk it will be harder on you!" Sherwood said to Greg.

Greg watched as the police car started rolling down the hill toward the river. Officer Sherwood turned around to see what Greg was laughing about, as the vehicle rolled toward the river.

"What the Hell!" Officer Sherwood cried as he ran after the car.

Greg felt his hands being untied. The rope fell behind him. He ran into the woods and headed for the road to the golf course above the Rocks.

CHAPTER FORTYSIX

Mikey and Greg

Greg crossed the road above the woods and headed into the golf course. Running across the green above the eighth hole, he entered his back yard. The back door to the house was locked but he had the key to the front. Greg walked slowly around the side stopping to look up and down the street.

He didn't think the policemen would be bothering him again tonight but he wasn't taking any chances. He climbed onto the porch from the side instead of walking up the front steps.

Opening the screen door Greg froze when he heard a voice speaking from the other end of the porch.

The Bookman was sitting on the porch glider in the shadows.

"Good evening Greg."

Greg walked over and sat down next to the Bookman.

"Mikey works for you in the bookstore."

"Yes."

"So what are you doing here?"

"Making sure you get this." The Bookman said."

"He handed Greg a bag. Inside there was a half- gallon of ice cream.

"It's what my brother wanted, Rocky Road!"

"Give some to Mikey when he gets here."

Greg opened the front door. When he turned to thank the Bookman there was no one there.

Mikey and Greg

An hour after Greg arrived home Mikey showed up on the front porch. He sat on the glider thinking. Thinking was one thing he could always do.

Most of time it got him into hot water but it also saved him from being grounded.

Being grounded in your room was one thing, but being grounded in the same room with Josh the mathematician was quite another thing.

Mikey kept telling his mother that if he had to be grounded in their bedroom at the same time Josh wouldn't get his math homework done. She let him go into the backyard until bedtime. Mikey would sit in the dark with his cigarette. Their landlord had a shed next to the alley. In case it rained he sat on the mattresses someone had thrown inside the shed.

One dark evening as Mikey spread himself on the mattresses he realized he was out of smokes.

"Damn!"

If he went back into the house to bum some smokes from Eric, his mother would have kittens. She wasn't due to leave for her night shift at the diner for another hour.

This was when he met Greg. The shed was open on the alley side. It was originally a place for lawn and garden tools. Mikey's mom and Eric weren't into growing flowers or grass, at least not the kind of grass you mowed every week in the summer.

Mikey was sitting on the mattresses when he heard a bike coming down the alley. The rider hit a pothole. Both the rider and the bike flew into the shed. The rider fell on the mattresses as the bike hit Mikey in the knee.

Groaning from pain Mikey kicked the bike away from him.

"Hey that's my bike!"

"And this is my knee which your bike almost broke."

"Oh hey sorry, OK? It was an accident."

Mikey didn't say anything. He sat and rubbed his knee.

"OK?" The boy asked.

"Yeah sure, OK," Mikey told him, "Aren't you in my brother's classroom?"

"Oh you mean Josh? You must be Mikey. I've heard about you."

"Not from Josh I hope."

"No, from my brother Tommy," Greg laughed, "You found him a dog, remember?"

"What's your name?"

"Greg."

"You're the kid who cares for his little brother?"

"We sort of take care of each other. Mom is kind of sick. Well, to be honest she just can't do what other mothers do, so Tommy and me we pitch in and take care of each other including our mom."

Greg brushed the grass clippings from his lap. "Mikey?"

"What is it Greg?"

"Thanks for getting that puppy for Tommy. Because of that dog I have more time to myself. Where did you get the dog anyway?"

"It's a long story Greg. Not now though. Hey! You got any fags?"

"Just so happens I do."

They smoked and talked. Mikey found out some amazing things about Greg as they sat together in the shed that night.

The Porch at Greg's House

"If I ring Greg's doorbell he won't see me. He has to know what happened to those cops and how their car ended up on the Rocks in the river. So Think Michael! I'm sitting on a porch that is in the third dimension but I am in the fourth dimension. I want to be in the third, which is safe to be in now, but how do I get there? Why is everything so complicated? I just wanted to go to North Carolina with mom and Eric. Go down to the Rocks to think, and look what happens?"

Mikey's cell phone vibrates in his pocket. "Your nickel is good. Go ahead nerds."

"We can't read your mind Mikey." Benjamin said.

"As if you have one we could read." Josh told him.

Mikey stood up and cried! "That's it! Quantum can put me back in the third dimension."

"We all saw you at the Rocks Mikey. Quantum couldn't show us what you were doing but we really enjoyed your special ballet in the grass."

"You know where I am now?"

"We see you on Greg's porch." Josh said. "That's why we called.

"May I speak to Quantum? I have to be in the third dimension before going inside Greg's house. We have to explain to him what happened down by the Rocks!"

"We are on a conference call with Quantum. Quantum has a report from the Village Police." Josh said.

"Quantum didn't have to draw us a picture Mikey." Benjamin laughed.

"The policemen were chasing a shop lifter who ran down to the rocks. As they grabbed him in the woods the police car moved downhill into the river. Officer Mitchell forgot to put the emergency brake on." Josh said.

Quantum spoke. "The satellite transmissions are very good tonight. What do you want me to do with you Mikey?"

"Guess we owe Greg an explanation Quantum."

"Do you suppose Greg will go to the farm with us?" Josh asked.

"Josh. I was going to stick with Mom and go with her and Eric to North Carolina."

"Mom will report us missing." Mikey said.

"Mikey. We have been missing for two days now and Mom hasn't reported us missing yet." Josh said.

"So? She works nights. Maybe she hasn't had time.

"Mikey. You are not a dummy. We were the ones who made sure that Children's Services didn't take us away from mom. Mom kept us only because she got a large check each month from the state to keep us out of foster care. You and I were what mom needed in order to have her druggie boy friends in bed with her." Josh told him.

"So you think we can leave here. Will she ever want us back again?" Mikey asked.

"So why did you go to the rocks Mikey instead of going to our house?"

"Can we do that Quantum? Can we leave and then come back?" Mikey asked.

"You can return to the third dimension Mikey. Once you reach the next dimension you will never want to live in the third dimension again. Trust me."

"Can I take a rain check on that Quantum?

Greg's Room

Mikey rang the bell to Greg's house. Greg's brother Tommy answered the door. Greg's brother was 10 years old. Sigmund, the brown lab puppy was six months old. He wagged his tail when Mikey entered. Tommy had a bowl of ice cream in his hand trying to keep it above the puppy as it tried to lick the bottom of the bowl.

"He's in his room." Tommy said.

'Where's your mom?"

"She's OK," Tommy said, "passed out on the couch hours ago."

Mikey saw that Tommy had covered his mom with a soft wool blanket and placed a pillow beneath her head."

Mikey started up the stairs.

"Guess we are lucky Mikey." Tommy said.

"What? Why?"

"We get to see our father one month each year."

"You mean when you visit him in New Jersey,?"

"Yeah."

"Greg says he takes good care of you guys.""

Sure Mikey. If we want a game boy or a Sony Play Station he sends it to us."

"Wish I had a father like you have Tommy."

"For one month we get to call him Dad."

"Better than what I got for a father Tommy."

"Mikey?"

"Yeah?"

"Thanks for Sigmund."

"No sweat kid."

As he entered Greg's room Mikey threw off his coat and shoes. Greg sat on the bed.

"You OK now Greg?" Mikey asked.

"You told them!" Greg cried.

"No Greg. I didn't"

"Then why did they pick me up and ask me about you?"

"They are after Josh and me. They will do anything to get us."

"So what's this all about?"

"Greg. You have the most sophisticated electronic set up in the whole village. Even the police department doesn't have one tenth the technology that's in this room."

"Thanks to my father. All this came here FED-EX, UPS and USPS. My dad takes good care of us. He sends us all the latest in computer technology."

"I know Greg. We set it up together. My brother and his friend Benjamin don't have any idea what is here in your room."

"You gave me your word you would never tell anyone about what I have here."

"What happened for you to think that I told anyone anything about what is in this room?"

"The man you work for in the store was on my porch when I came back from the Rocks. He knows about us."

Mikey put his index fingers on each side of his temples.

"You told him about this room."

"The Bookman was here on your porch?"

"That's the person."

"Mikey sat back on the bed and relaxed.

"That man in the store where you work Mikey."

"He was here, like in your house?"

"On the porch when I ran home."

Then when Greg explained what happened to him during the previous hours, Mikey told Greg about the Secret Room.

"Remember the night we met in the alley, in the shed, Mikey?"

"What about it?"

"My father told me that our work on the computers was going to result in new dimensions. He told me that we would be travelling out west to a special place.

The cops pick me up to ask questions about you, Josh and this guy Benjamin. They were going to waste me if I didn't tell them where you were Mikey."

"Then what did they do?"

"Then, when the cop car rolled down the hill something or someone untied me."

"That is an interesting story Greg. What were you doing at the Rocks?"

"How did you know I was at the Rocks?" Greg asked.

"It's time to meet Quantum." Mikey told him.

CHAPTER FOURTYSEVEN

Benjamin's Place

Four future space travelers were sitting in the kitchen.

"Now that you know about us, what are we going to do?" Mikey asked.

"Why did you bring Greg and his brother Tommy here?" Josh asked him.

Benjamin walked into the room. "You never told us about Greg Mikey. You were in Greg's room with the best of the best!"

Mikey looked at Benjamin and his brother Josh. "His father sent all this equipment Josh. Benjamin?"

"FED-EX, UPS?"

"And USPS" Tommy said.

"Mikey promised not to tell anyone." Greg told them. "My father sends anything we want. He sends us money. My mother gets a check every month to take care of us and she gets money from social security for herself."

Mikey spoke up. "Greg takes care of his brother and his mother."

"So no one but you and Tommy knew that she is passed out every day after dinner?" Mikey asked Greg, knowing the answer.

"We learned how to cook." Tommy said.

"What about shopping for food?" Josh asked. "Didn't anyone ask you where your mom was?" Benjamin asked.

"Mikey showed us how to get the groceries Ben without others being suspicious."

Josh put his hands above him. "Don't tell me! My brother enlisted the help of Eric to take you to the store. He drove you home with the bags of groceries? Am I right so far?"

Greg looked at Mikey. "Your brother doesn't know Mikey?"

Josh sat down. "Mikey is good at keeping secrets! What did you have to pay Eric for doing this?"

"We bought his cigarettes for him." Greg told him.

"Why do you think we always had enough smokes to go around Josh?" Mickey asked.

Silence filled the room.

"So where did you guys learn how to cook?" Benjamin asked.

"We watched the food channel." Greg replied. "We lived on peanut butter and jelly sandwiches until Mikey came along."

Josh glared at Mikey. "You kept secrets from me!" He cried.

"Sure. What are brothers for Josh?" Mikey told him. "Besides, a promise is a promise."

"Mikey! I'm in the bedroom working over these books, thinking you are in the shed in the back yard, when all the time you are over at Greg's helping him set up all these electronic shipments from UPS and FEDEX!"

"And don't forget USPS." Tommy said reaching for another of Mrs. Fontana's cookies.

"Jeez!"

Benjamin grabbed Josh by the arm.

"Can you guys stay here while we decide what to do? Stay here while we go upstairs. "Give Sigmund another cookie Tommy."

Benjamin and Josh left the kitchen and headed upstairs to Benjamin's room.

Josh sat on the floor. Benjamin flopped on the bed and put his face in a pillow.

After a few moments they both started laughing hysterically.

Finally, when they stopped laughing Josh said, "None of us can explain to Greg what happened to the police car."

"Greg doesn't even think that it was strange when the car rolled down the hill and his ropes were cut loose."

"We need to let Mikey explain to Greg why he wasn't there when he was there." Benjamin said.

"What do you think Greg has in his room?" Josh asked.

"Maybe we can ask Quantum." Benjamin suggested.

"Quantum will know every device hooked up to Greg's computer."

"He knows. Greg E-mailed the Bookman's computer."

"Who is Greg's father in New Jersey? What if he rats on us?"

"We can take this a step at a time, as Grandfather says."

"Ben, are you thinking what I'm thinking?"

"That Greg and Tommy's father is the Mountain Man?"

CHAPTER FORTYEIGHT

Greg Enters the Secret Room

"So you are the computer who has been sending E-Mail to me?" Greg

asked Quantum.

"What do you think of this room?" Quantum asked.

"You didn't answer my question." Greg said.

"Yes. When your father delivered and set up the system in your room you

became part of our project on the network." Quantum hummed and clicked.

"My father connected my system to his quantum physics research projects

at Princeton?"

"Yes." Quantum replied.

"This room is awesome. Are we on some kind of spaceship?"

"This is the Spaceship Earth Greg."

"If you are a quantum computer then you must know my father."

"He is the Chief Aerospace Engineer of our project."

**Greg laughed. That's all he ever talks about in his E-Mails except
asking about mom, Tommy and me, and how we are doing in school."**

"The sunflower is our symbol. Each day it begins by facing the rising sun

in the east. Then the sunflower follows the light across the sky turning to the west as the sun sets. My father said that the Sunflower spacecraft is designed

from the shape of the sunflower seed." **Greg told Quantum.**

"You know a lot about the project."

"Will the Sunflower travel to a new dimension from this room?" Greg
asked.

"From the Earth's moon Greg." Mikey said.

"It will launch from the Dark Side of the Moon!" Josh added.

CHAPTER FOURTYNINE

Quantum Speaks to Benjamin

"Benjamin you know we are all going to the Farm?"

"How are we going to get there?" Benjamin asked.

"We have reservations on Amtrak's 'Capital Limited'. This train runs from Washington D.C. to Chicago's Union Station." Quantum explained.

"Where do we get on this train? How many of us? Benjamin asked.

"Everyone is going!" Quantum buzzed and clicked. "I reserved a sleeping car for all of us at the end of the train."

"Josh, Mikey, Greg, Tommy and my mom and Gianna?" Benjamin smiled.

Quantum put a happy face on the large monitor.

"What about Tommy's dog Sigmund?" Benjamin added.

"There is plenty of room for dogs on our farm. Sigmund will have to travel in the baggage car. Tommy will be allowed to visit him there." Quantum assured him.

"What about Greg's mom?"

"She will be flown to Oregon and enter a hospital where her family can visit her."

"How will your Aerospace Engineer travel?"

"We board the train in Pittsburgh. A special car is coming from Princeton Junction and will be attached to The Capitol Limited. Greg's father will be on this car with me." Quantum told him.

"Quantum is this special car going to be invisible?"

"It will be Benjamin, all the way to the Chicago rail yard and all the way to Portland, Oregon." Quantum hummed.

Federal Marshal Gaylord Gray

Marshal Gray entered Chief Fairchild's office.

"Welcome to our village." The Chief said. "What brings you here all the way from our nation's capital?"

"Our National Defense agency has received information concerning unusual phenomena and unusual criminal activity occurring in you village."

"What kind of information Marshal?"

"You have an Officer Sherwood who contacted us at the National Crime Information Center. The NCIC people passed this information on to my office."

"We don't take anything Officer Sherwood has to say, seriously." The Chief laughed.

"Ordinarily our office does not deal with information concerning people who vanish into thin air. In this case it may involve an organization we have been after for many years. Officer Sherwood is convinced that he is not to be blamed for recent unexplainable mysterious attacks by invisible persons."

The Chief listened carefully to what the Marshal was telling him.

"In addition to receiving this information from a member of your department, there have been accusations of serious criminal activity involving your department."

"What are these allegations and who are the parties responsible for making them?" The Chief demanded to know.

"Federal agents will be here soon. They will contact you with all of the necessary facts resulting from the investigations Chief. Meanwhile my marshals and I will pursue and capture these invisible people."

CHAPTER FIFTY

Pawn Man Meets the Marshal

The Marshall opened his wallet displaying the badge. He let the Pawn Man exam his ID with his photo on it.

"That picture was taken a long time ago." The Pawn Man squinted.

Carefully the Marshal folded his wallet and sat on one of the Pawn Man's stools.

Turning slowly away from the Pawn Man the Marshall looked across the street toward the Bookstore.

"So what can I do for you?" The Pawn man asked him.

"We want to take pictures."

"What pictures Marshal?"

"Pictures of people going in and out of that bookstore across the street." The Marshal said.

"Not from my shop you're not. My customers would freak out."

"You have any books at home?" The Marshal asked.

"I don't read books so I don't have any at home." He told the Marshal.

"What if we decided to bring in the IRS boys to take a look at your books? Would you change your mind and let us take our pictures?"

"Your IRS boys are welcome to audit my books."

"What about the books in your safe at home?" The Marshal asked.

"By the time they get to my house there won't be any books in my safe." The Pawn man told him."

"I'm afraid it's too late."

"What do you mean Marshal?"

"The search warrants were issued this morning. The agents are at your house as we speak."

"Take all the pictures you want. You won't find anything wrong over there."

In The Secret Room

Grandfather entered the room when Gianna turned the shower handle.

"We are leaving tonight. Everyone is ready and packed for the flight to Pittsburgh."

Quantum performed a final check on the trains. "The Capitol Limited will arrive in Pittsburgh three hours late." Quantum announced.

"What about the car being attached in Princeton Junction? Will it arrive at the end of Amtrack's Pennsylvanian in time to hook onto the Capitol train?" Benjamin asked.

Josh pointed to a monitor showing the routes of both trains.

"Quantum delayed the Capitol Limited on its way up from Maryland."

"Quantum made connections with a Canadian Pacific freight system computer which caused the delay with our train." Josh continued to explain.

"You will all arrive in Union Station at midnight and board the train to Chicago." Quantum told them. "Your flight is scheduled to leave from here at 2100 hours. Everyone will leave for the Pittsburgh airport accept Greg's mother who will fly to Denver with a connection to Portland." Quantum said.

The door to the room opened with a grind.

Mikey came running up the stairs.

"Quantum. everybody! We are in real trouble."

"What is it Mikey?" Grandfather asked.

"The Marshal is in town!"

"HI HO!" Quantum cried. "There is to be a gunfight at OK Corral."

"Quantum, how could you let this happen? You were able to control the files in The National Security System." Benjamin asked surprised.

"That is exactly what we did Benjamin. We sent information to the National Security Computers." Quantum told him.

"But why would you do that?"

"To create chaos and mass confusion while we make our escape to the farm."

"What's going to happen?" Josh asked.

"Tomorrow Federal Agents will seize Lieutenant Frank's Computer from his home. It has a few thousand pictures they will be interested in." Quantum said.

"Kiddy porn?" Josh asked.

"That and worse Josh. He videotaped the teen ager's death in the village jail and stored it on his hard drive. The man who hung himself later on is also one of Lieutenant Frank's video stars. Amazing what you can find in some people's computers."

"Eric told me they were called 'Snuff' movies." Josh said.

"Snuff to put the Lieutenant in a cell of his own for a long time." Mikey said.

"What else did you tell the Federal Agents Quantum?" Benjamin asked.

"We gave them the hiding place of the Pawn Man's record books and his cash."

"What about the cops?" Mikey wanted to know.

"The Federal agents will be spending a few weeks in the village going through the court and police records." Quantum told them.

"Quantum we have to get out of this place! Mikey cried.

CHAPTER FIFTYONE

Marshal Gray

The Marshal called for a strategy meeting in the Chief's office. Officer Sherwood and Officer Mitchell joined the Marshal. Both policemen were nervous as they sat on the couch.

"Our search team is requesting your help rounding up everyone involved in the events you reported Officer Sherwood.

"We have searched the entire village Marshal." Sherwood told him.

"So where are those people?" The Marshal demanded.

"Our department has not been able to find any of them sir."

"In other words officers, they are hiding?"

"No. We don't think so. The mother of two of the boys and her boyfriend have left town. She probably took her sons with her." Officer Mitchel replied.

"Probably, but you are not certain Officer?"

"No one saw any of them packing their car and leaving. We questioned the neighbors." Sherwood added.

"What about the other boy and his mother?" Marshal Gray was angry.

"Not only have they packed up and left, the lady living downstairs is gone too."

"Has this department of incompetents notified the department of motor vehicles? Or don't you keep records here of automobiles and the registration numbers?"

"The police bulletins we sent out have all that information Marshal. We don't just eat donuts here." Mitchell fired back at the Marshal.

"Easy Mitch the Marshal is just doing his job." Sherwood cautioned.

"There is another boy and his brother who live in the village? Didn't you have some problems with him last week?" The Marshal asked.

"We checked his place." Sherwood told him.

"Don't tell me," the marshal said sarcastically, no one was home?"

"They have gone to ground along with their mother."

"And of course no one saw them leave either." Marshal Gray said pretending to be surprised.

"One of their neighbors reports that the mother was taken from the house on Tuesday evening by a man with a beard. They didn't see her sons get into the car."

"Again you have no license registration or make of the car?"

"Yes. We are not that incompetent. The car was found at the airport last night. We checked the airline reservations." The Chief replied smiling.

"So you officers do know how to investigate. Where were their reservations taking them?"

"Pittsburgh. The trail ended there as there were no connections to other flights."

"You searched all three houses carefully?"

"Yes. We conducted a thorough search. All of them are gone."

"My team is looking inside of each of the houses as we speak." The Marshal said. "We shall see how carefully you looked."

"The only evidence we found was a plate of chocolate chip cookies Marshal." Sherwood confessed.

"And where are these cookies?"

Officer Mitchell turned red. "We ate them sir."

"Not we Mitch, you!" Sherwood cried.

"Which leaves us with one more place to investigate officers?"

The Marshal Continues to Investigate

The Marshal's team found nothing by searching the homes where the boys lived. He had them set up road blocks leading from the village even though he did not expect to find any of them. Marshals were sent to the airport in Pittsburgh in hopes of discovering their destination.

Officer Sherwood spoke with excitement.

"Of course we haven't searched the Bookstore!"

"It appears that that bookstore is the center of this whole conspiracy." The Marshal told them.

"Now what are we going to do?" Officer Sherwood asked.

"You two will back me up, one at the front door and one of you at the side door. I am going in and arrest that Bookman for the interrogation of his life."

Marshal Gray left the Chief's office and crossed the village street.

As the three of them surrounded the bookstore Officer Sherwood spoke to the Marshal.

"What if that punk teenager is in there Marshal? Do we take him too?"

"You officers can have that teenager while we interrogate the man in the Bookstore."

"This should be great!" Officer Mitchell said.

"And this is a legal raid?" Sherwood asked.

"Haven't you heard about the Patriot Act?" The Marshal asked.

"We haven't kept up with the new Federal Laws in our little village." Mitchell told him sarcastically.

"Easy Mitch, we are on a mission here." Sherwood told him.

"From what we can see, coming to this God-Forsaken Village, you guys can't even keep up with your own laws let alone constitutional law."

"We run a clean town here Marshal." Sherwood said.

"What is so clean about it officer?"

"Do you see any Blacks in this village Marshal?"

"Now that you mention it, I haven't."

"So let's go across the street and get this pervert!"

As the officers took up their positions Marshal Gray entered the shop of books.

Bells jingled above him. Angels got their wings.

"May we help you sir?"

"Where is the man who owns this place?"

"You are speaking to him sir."

"Not you, the older man who was here yesterday." The Marshal told him.

"There was no one else here yesterday."

"He was here. I was talking to him."

"How very extraordinary since I was the only one here yesterday."

The Marshal walked to the rear of the store.

"They escaped me! They escaped from me again!" He cried.

CHAPTER FIFTYTWO

AMTRAK – The Capitol Limited – Pittsburgh Union Station

The Amtrak train backed into the station in the darkness of the night. It arrived in the steel city three hours late, unusual for the Capitol Limited.

The porters on the platform waited for the baggage car to stop. When the train halted they were not standing next to the baggage and mail car.

"The train engineer stopped one car short of us." One of the porters said.

"Move up to the next car." His supervisor told him. The Capitol probably has an extra car at the end."

The porters pushed their carts ahead and began loading them into the baggage car.

"Where do you want us to put this dog?" They asked the train man.

Suddenly three boys stepped into the baggage car from behind.

"Put the dog over here by me. Looks like a real nice Labrador man" The trainman said to them.

Sigmund wagged his tail as Tommy approached the cage. "We are going to the Farm."

"Get back to your car." The train man ordered. "You can come up here once we get underway."

Greg ushered his brother to the rear of the baggage car where they walked through the train, to their sleeper car.

Finally Greg said to his brother, "Tommy you got to keep all of this to yourself. There could be people on this train who don't want us to get to the farm."

The Capitol Limited pulled out of the station and headed across the river on the way to Chicago.

The Train Man questioned why a baggage car was coupled ahead of a first class sleeper car. He knew nothing about the last car on the train following the sleeper.

The Capitol Limited was carrying the Sunflower Travelers, along with an invisible hitch hiker. Quantum hummed and clicked in the unseen railcar.

****

End Book I - <u>Sunflower Chronicles</u> - **The Secret Room**

www.ingramcontent.com/pod-product-compliance
Lightning Source LLC
Chambersburg PA
CBHW062021170626
46813CB00001B/251